MADNESS

ALSO BY **ZAC BREWER**

The Cemetery Boys
The Blood Between Us

THE CHRONICLES OF VLADIMIR TOD
Eighth Grade Bites
Ninth Grade Slays
Tenth Grade Bleeds
Eleventh Grade Burns
Twelfth Grade Kills

THE SLAYER CHRONICLES
First Kill
Second Chance
Third Strike

The Legacy of Tril: Soulbound

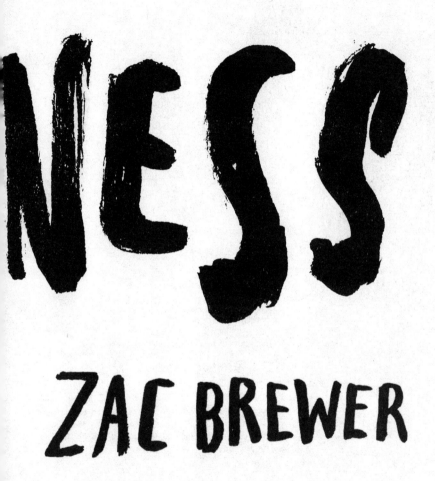

NESS

ZAC BREWER

HARPERTEEN
An Imprint of HarperCollinsPublishers

HarperTeen is an imprint of HarperCollins Publishers.

Madness
Copyright © 2017 by Zac Brewer
www.epicreads.com

ISBN 978-0-06-245785-1

Typography by Carla Weise
This book is set in 12-point Filosofia
17 18 19 20 21   PC/LSCH   10 9 8 7 6 5 4 3 2 1
❖
First Edition

To my husband, Paul,
for always being that hand in the darkness

AUTHOR'S NOTE

If, as you are reading this book, you find yourself experiencing symptoms of depression or suicidal thoughts, please seek help. You are not alone. And you can recover.

Below are but a few of the great many resources available to you.

For more information on depression and how to get help, visit the Youth Resources page of the American Academy of Childhood and Adolescent Psychiatry (AACAP). There you'll find information on finding the right care for yourself, how to recognize depression in others, and what you can do to help someone in crisis. www.aacap.org

For further educational resources—as well as inspirational stories of recovery—visit To Write Love on Her Arms. TWLOHA is a nonprofit movement dedicated to finding help for people struggling with depression, addiction, self-injury, and suicide. www.twloha.com

The National Suicide Prevention Lifeline exists to provide immediate assistance to individuals in suicidal crisis by connecting them to the nearest available suicide prevention and mental health service provider through a toll-free number. 1-800-273-TALK (8255)

If you are in immediate crisis, dial 911.

The world is a better place with you in it.

The course of true love never did run smooth.

—WILLIAM SHAKESPEARE

Love is like war: easy to begin but very hard to stop.

—H. L. MENCKEN

When love is not madness, it is not love.

—PEDRO CALDERÓN DE LA BARCA

CHAPTER ONE

"It's a different color for you."

My mom was speaking with the same overly chipper tone she'd been using since she'd picked me up a few hours ago. She was trying to come off as supportive, but it was really ringing through my ears as fake. It was all fake. My new hair color, our casual conversation, the fact that I'd been released from Kingsdale Hospital with a "not crazy" stamp of approval. And I knew a thing or two about fake. I'd faked my way through six weeks of treatment with all the right words to all the right people. I'd convinced them all that I was in full-on recovery mode after what happened six weeks ago. But it was a lie. I was just trying to get out of that place, away from those white, sterile walls, even though I had no idea what it would be like once I did.

I only knew that I felt like a failure.

Staring out the window as Mom barreled down I-75 in the direction of our home, I thought about how, in a way, my life *had* ended that night in Black River. This—whatever this was—wasn't life. It was my afterlife.

"Yeah," I said. For seventeen years I'd had waves of strawberry-blond hair that hung to my waist. An hour ago, I'd had it dyed pink ombre. Part of me knew that I'd chosen that color to shove and poke at my mom's overly supportive act. She'd never let me dye my hair before. It had been an ongoing argument between us since I was thirteen. After four years of arguments, what had changed that suddenly made a surprise trip to the salon okay? Did she think that giving in to this one thing would somehow take back the guilt she might have over what happened? Ridiculous. So I'd chosen the most off-kilter color I could think of. I didn't even like pink. Or pastels.

Mom's phone buzzed as a text came through. To my annoyance, she picked it up with her right hand and continued steering with her left. I hated when she played with her phone while driving. It was so dangerous. People should never text and drive.

The irony that I was concerned about her endangering my life hit me hard, like a slap across the cheek. What did it matter whether I'd drowned that night or smashed into a semitruck now because my mom refused to put her phone down while operating a vehicle? What made this so different from that?

Because, I told myself, *the river was my choice.* This was hers. And at least I wouldn't have taken anyone else down with me when I jumped into that water. It was just me. Just my ending. No one else's.

Mom said, "It's Ronald, wanting to know if you're up for seeing him this evening."

She and my dad were the only people on the planet who still called my best friend since kindergarten Ronald. Sure, it was his name. But ever since we watched that John Hughes movie *Pretty in Pink* together in sixth grade, he'd been Duckie to me. After a while he was Duckie to everyone. Just not my parents.

"I don't want to see anybody." I slid down in my seat a little. It was embarrassing. I was embarrassed. Not for having attempted to take my life. But for having failed. "I'm not ready."

She paused, biting her bottom lip, forcing down words that she clearly wanted to say. She started typing on her phone with her thumb before she even spoke again to me.

"Okay. I'll tell him." Her words were breathy and made me wonder what she was telling him exactly. My phone hadn't yet been returned to me, or I would have asked him. Of course, if I'd had my phone, Duckie would've just texted me directly.

She cleared her throat and said, "I think you should know, I've kept Ronald informed about your situation—"

Situation. Right. That's what it was. Just a situation. Nothing more.

"—so he's fully aware of your diagnosis and the treatment you're undergoing. I just . . . I just thought it might be good to have a friend involved."

Involved? Or an extra pair of eyes on me?

I'd thought about Duckie a lot since the doctors had given me a release date. I wondered what he thought about what I did, if he was mad at me for not telling him I wanted to die, why he hadn't come to see me on visitors' day. I was glad he hadn't come. I didn't want to have to smile at Duckie the way I smiled at my parents, the way I smiled at the doctors and nurses, the way I smiled all through the last few days of inpatient treatment. The truth was, I'd smiled my way out of the last six weeks at that damn hospital but hadn't made any real progress. The truth was, I still wanted to die.

But I wasn't about to share that bit of information with anyone.

I'd learned early on during my stay in Kingsdale that their staff had pretty amazing bullshit detectors. If you tried to make light of things too soon, they only probed deeper, through the veil of your lies, to find the truth. I'd kept my mouth shut for the first week and observed. Then, slowly, I'd begun to act as if I were opening up, then growing hopeful, then regretful that I had thrown myself in the river. Eventually I convinced them that I was ready to face the world and wanted to change. I guess their bullshit detectors were off with me. I just wanted to be alone again so I could finish what I started. I just wanted to be free. Of the hospital. Of the pain. Of my life.

Dark stuff, maybe. But that didn't make it any less true.

My mom cleared her throat. It was as if she were attempting small talk with a stranger. Maybe she was. "Do you want anything from Starbucks?"

"Can we go home now, please?" I flicked the buckle on my backpack back and forth, not meeting her eyes.

She seemed relieved at my response. Maybe she wanted the tension in the car to evaporate and knew that going home would shorten our time alone together. Maybe I was way off base and she was glad I was engaging in conversation with her—brief as it was. I didn't feel compelled to ask, and I was tired of analyzing. I just wanted to get the initial steps of my return home over with already.

As we climbed a hill, I could make out Black River in the distance. I couldn't see the stone bridge, not from here, but it was there.

Instantly, I was transported back in time. I was seven years old. My dad was teaching me how to swim. As my head went under, I gulped in water, flailing my arms. I surfaced again, choking, and my dad pulled me out onto the deck of the pool. He looked so disappointed, so annoyed that I hadn't done it right the first time. He said, "There's no reason to panic, Brooke. It's impossible to drown yourself."

But Dad had been wrong. With enough Tylenol PM, it was easy enough. In fact, if the old man who'd pulled me from the water hadn't seen me jump, I wouldn't be sitting in my mom's SUV now, still hurting with a pain that I couldn't explain or ease or wish away. I'd be gone. Somewhere better, maybe. Maybe nowhere at all. Just not here.

I reached inside my backpack and pulled out the prescription bottle with my name on it. The rattling of the pills inside briefly caught my mom's attention. She bit her bottom lip. I ignored her. The pills were white, with a black stripe and a green stripe wrapped around them. The doctors had called them antidepressants. They'd said that it might take several tries to find the right medication, the right dose. I was pretty sure they were full of shit. But I'd taken the pills at Kingsdale. Mostly because they watched me take them every day. I wondered if my parents would take over watching me from now on.

As I dropped the bottle back inside my bag, I looked at the three pink lines that marked my left arm. I hadn't been trying to reach my veins, to slash my wrists, to die in such a bloody way. It wasn't suicide then. Not yet. That was months before the night on the bridge. I'd just wanted to feel . . . something. Anything. Even if that thing was pain.

Of course, I was a total coward and couldn't get up the guts to do that right the first time, either. I'd downed some of Dad's scotch and tossed a couple of Mom's Vicodin and dulled the pain that I was longing to feel. Pretty stupid of me in hindsight. Made the whole thing pointless. Not that the experience had held much point anyway.

Word of advice: skin isn't easy to cut into. Not even with a brand-new box cutter. Not even when you apply a lot of pressure. I managed a few scratches at first. It stung, even through the dulling assistance of pills and booze. So I reached for one of my dad's chef's knives and resorted to sawing at my skin with its razor-sharp edge, pressing hard into my flesh until crimson bloomed. There wasn't a lot of blood, despite all my hard work and determination. And in the end I was left with three small scars on my arm—scars I explained away to anyone who asked as a clumsy accident tripping into tools in the garage. No one pushed the issue after I explained. Not even Duckie.

The cuts had healed relatively quickly and had already begun to fade. But even if they faded entirely with time, they would always be there in my memory. Scars don't ever disappear—not really.

Mom turned the wheel, and we moved onto a familiar road. Two more turns and we were approaching our house. My stomach shrank painfully inside of me. I had hoped never to see this place again. I had planned everything so well. I'd thought I had, anyway. But I hadn't planned on some nosy old man being out digging for night crawlers. I hadn't planned on a stranger intervening in the moment I'd been dreaming of, counting on for months.

We pulled into the driveway and "The Sound of Silence" by Disturbed came on over the radio. Mom killed the engine, cutting off the melancholy tune. For a moment, I didn't move. I didn't feel sad or angry. I really didn't feel anything at all—apart from the determination to finish what I'd started at Black River. I was going to get it right the moment an opportunity presented itself. And no one—not my parents, not Duckie, not some stupid old man—was going to stop me.

With a deep breath, I opened the car door. After I grabbed my suitcase from the backseat, I followed Mom up the front walk. The flowers out front had bloomed while I was in treatment. Shades of red, orange, and yellow greeted me as I made my way to the door with my backpack slung over my shoulder and suitcase in my hand. Their colors reminded me of flames.

Stepping inside the front door was like moving back in time. The floral paper covering the walls of the foyer seemed foreign to me, like something I'd once encountered in a dream. In fact, that's what the entire experience felt like: a bad dream.

I stared at the hands on the grandfather clock for a moment before moving deeper into the house. Time felt like it was dragging on, digging its claws in. My dad was sitting in his chair in the living room, reading the paper. When Mom spoke, her voice was more chipper than ever, bordering on shrill. "Look who's home, dear!"

Dad glanced up from his paper, but not at me. At the space between me and where Mom was standing. "Need help with your bags?"

He looked older, somehow, even though I'd just seen him two weeks before on visitors' day. The lines in his face seemed deeper. He slouched in his chair. I wondered if he was glad that I was home, but didn't dare ask. Shaking my head, I said, "No. I can manage."

With a crinkle of newsprint, Dad went back to reading his paper without another word. I was more relieved than disappointed. Maybe this was his afterlife too. Just a blank haze of existence. An impending feeling of "get on with it already." Nothing more.

Mom shuffled her feet a little, wringing her hands as she stared at Dad. I didn't know what she'd expected him to do, greet me with hugs and smiles, balloons and a Welcome Back banner? Frankly, I was glad I didn't have to face a conversation with him about what I'd done. I was far more comfortable with his silence than I was with Mom's false optimism. At least Dad was keeping it real. He was upset. And that was okay.

I carried my bags upstairs—each step seemed to make them just a bit heavier. When I reached the top, I looked down the hall to my bedroom door. The hall felt longer than I remembered, and as I moved toward my room, it felt like the distance lengthened with every step I took. The motion felt strange, wrong. Uneven, somehow.

I stretched out my hand and curled my fingers around the doorknob. Turning it slowly, I heard the click of the mechanism as it released. With a gentle push, my bedroom door swung open. My heart sank deep inside of me, down to that dark place I'd called normal for so long.

The old man's words whispered through my mind— the ones he'd spoken as he held me there on the riverbank after he'd pulled me from the frigid water, as the faint cry of approaching sirens grew. "You'll be okay, sweetheart. Everything's going to be just fine."

He was wrong. I wasn't okay then, and I still wasn't now. But I would be soon. Because now—more than ever—I was determined to die.

CHAPTER TWO

Holding my breath, I flipped on the light switch.

Apart from how obvious it was that my parents had raided my room while I was inpatient to remove anything they deemed dangerous, pretty much everything was as I'd left it. I'd spent the day before my attempt cleaning so it would be nice when my parents saw it. Less work for them. With a glance, on the surface the room seemed put together and normal. But if you looked closer, underneath the bed, in the closet, you'd see the mess. It was a lie. And I was a liar.

I set my suitcase beside my closed closet door and dropped my backpack on the floor next to it. I was trying not to get caught up in the waves of nostalgia and memories that washed over me once I was standing in my room. It was just a room, after all. Just a place to sleep. Nothing more. But then my eyes fell on the quilt that was so carefully smoothed out on my bed and my indifference dissolved into thin air. The quilt was old, hand sewn by my grandmother when she was only twelve years old. It was the first quilt that she'd ever made, and she'd created it under my great-grandmother's careful watch. I knew because she'd told me tons of stories about learning how to quilt—always with a bit of a sad glint in her eye. She'd never had a daughter to teach, and I wasn't exactly skilled with anything remotely crafty. As proven by the time I was ten and hot-glued the sleeve of the sweater I'd been wearing to my desk.

It must have been disappointing to her, to have enjoyed a task so much with her mother but not be able to pass it on. I'd often wondered if that had been a regret she'd carried into death.

The quilt was multicolored, but mostly purples and blues. The pattern was something she'd called a garden pattern. It looked like my bed was home to a hundred flowers. But not in an obnoxious, overly girly way. And even if it had been, I would have kept it on my bed.

I retrieved the bottle of medication and a paper origami crane from my backpack before lying down on my bed and closing my eyes. The quilt was soft against my skin. Soft like Grandma had always felt. Almost fragile, the way that her mind had become when Alzheimer's tightened its grip on her. She spent her last weeks in a hospital room. The final week they removed her feeding tube so that she'd starve to death. I never went to say good-bye. It was a decision that I still felt conflicted over.

I set the bottle beside me on the bed and held up the paper crane, pinching one of its tiny, stark white wings between my fingers. In the hospital, as part of my group therapy, the doctors taught us ways to distract ourselves from suicidal thoughts. Origami was apparently supposed to be extremely calming and helpful in this endeavor, but looking at the crane only reminded me of Joy.

She was in my therapy group. There were six of us, but Joy stood out. Mostly because she didn't seem afraid of the doctors or counselors. She didn't strike me as sad or alone, just determined to end herself. I admired that, even though I probably shouldn't have.

Joy had been in Kingsdale twice for suicide attempts. The first time she'd tried downing a fifth of vodka and a bottle of sleeping pills. The second time she'd swallowed everything in her parents' medicine cabinet. I'd asked her once if she ever thought about trying again. She'd whispered to me, "Third time's a charm."

We'd sit there in group, answer questions about ways we could deal with our emotions, and then it was origami time. Joy only ever made cranes. On her last day, she handed me the crane she'd just made and repeated her words: "Third time's a charm."

I wasn't sure what she meant by it. Not until I walked into the common area that afternoon and saw a buzz of doctors and nurses flitting about, shouting things. Joy was lying on her back on the white tile floor. Her large, dark eyes were open, but there was no spark of life in them. She was dead.

She didn't look scared. She didn't look lost or lonely. She looked at peace. I envied her that. It was all I ever wanted. Peace.

I could see blood on the tile, but nothing to indicate where it had come from. An orderly pushed me into my room and closed the door, standing in front of my small window and blocking my view. On my tiptoes, I managed to see Joy being placed on a stretcher and hurried away. Various staff members stood in front of the other patients' doors as well. We were on lockdown.

I slept heavy that night, but only because everyone was given a dose of something to keep the entire ward calm. When I awoke, I realized I was still holding the crane that Joy had given me. One of its tiny wings had a small bit of dried blood on the tip. I wondered if it was Joy's or mine.

The staff kept an even closer eye on all of us after that. Bedroom doors had to remain open. Trips to the bathroom were escorted. I didn't say much about anything at first, but all I really wanted to do was ask how Joy had died. I kept to myself for about a week, before slowly acting as if I were becoming open to the idea of therapy. It was the only way out, after all. I kept the crane, though. It felt somehow symbolic. Of Joy's triumph. Of my goal.

I zoned out in the familiar comfort of my bed, and eventually I must have fallen asleep, though I hadn't intended to. The one thing the meds did do was make me sleepy. Only I never dreamed. Or if I did have dreams, I didn't recall them. When I opened my eyes, morning light filtered into my room through the sheer curtains. I'd slept for over twelve hours. My fingers were curled gently around the crane, cupping it in my hand without crushing it. Familiar sorrow washed over me. I'd woken up. Again.

I sat up, knocking the bottle of pills to the floor as I swung my feet over the edge of the bed. After retrieving some thread and a thumbtack from my desk drawer, I hung the crane above my bed as a reminder. Once it was hung, I took a deep breath and headed for the door. I could already smell bacon and eggs, which meant that Mom was downstairs cooking and wouldn't notice what I was doing.

Behind me, the crane whispered its support. It knew I was making a new plan. One that would succeed. Just like Joy's had.

The hall seemed its normal length this morning, and I moved silently down it and past the stairs to my parents' bedroom. Before stepping inside, I listened carefully to make sure that no one was upstairs with me. After determining I had the floor to myself, I moved as quietly as I could through their bedroom over that god-awful mauve carpeting and into the master bath. Above the sink was a medicine cabinet. Inside would be the answer to my problem—life being the problem, of course.

I stepped in front of the sink, and the floor creaked slightly. Cursing inside my mind, I opened the cabinet, and my heart sank. A single bottle of some herbal headache medicine, a half-used tube of Bengay, and a box of Q-tips were the only things inside. Closing the mirror door, I searched the drawers of the cabinet below. Cotton balls, a hair dryer, a bottle of my mom's favorite moisturizer—nothing that would aid me. It was as if the place had been cleaned out.

No. No, that's exactly what had happened. Can't trust someone who's made an attempt on their life with anything sharper than a Q-tip or a cotton ball, now can we?

With a heavy sigh, I descended the stairs. This was going to be harder than I'd thought.

My dad was probably already gone for the day, so it was just Mom and me. Or so I thought, until I rounded the arched door that led to the kitchen. Mom was at the stove, flipping bacon in a sizzling pan. Duckie was sitting at the counter. He was the same Duckie I had left behind—his eyes intensely green, his hair brown with blond highlights and spiked up in a faux-hawk. He was dressed in bright colors in that mismatched way that said he didn't give a damn what anybody thought about him, so let 'em talk. He was the same Duckie. But I wasn't the same Brooke. There was a huge space between us before he even noticed I'd entered the room. I put it there.

He looked up at me in surprise, dropping a half-eaten triangle of buttered toast on his plate. His surprise quickly turned apologetic. "Hey, Brooke."

My mom shut down the stove and put the rest of the bacon on a plate. She turned around and smiled brightly at me, pretending that everything was normal. Probably in an effort to wish it that way. She'd always been like that. No matter how dark the skies got, she'd insist the sun was shining.

When I was little, she taught me to watch the sky fade from day to night. According to my mom, the first star to appear was a lucky one. And if you saw it, you could make a wish on it. She even taught me what to say to make my wish come true. "Star light, star bright, first star I see tonight. I wish I may, I wish I might, have the wish I wish tonight." None of my wishes ever came true. As I took the seat next to Duckie at the counter, I wondered if any of hers did.

She set the plate in front of me and said, "I heard you moving around upstairs. Looking for anything in particular?"

Damn creaky floor. I shrugged as nonchalantly as I could manage. "Just pain meds. I have a monster headache. Probably the stress of going back to school."

"We have some herbal headache medicine."

I noticed. "Herbs won't help me."

She sighed and straightened her shoulders as she looked at me. I knew this version of my mother. It was the face of the disciplinarian—a face she rarely wore. "Well, then I suggest you try closing your eyes and relaxing. All medication but Tylenol, Pepto-Bismol, and the like have been removed, just like the doctors told us. The liquor cabinet has been emptied, and anything sharp—including kitchen knives—have been hidden and locked away."

"What if I want to cut up veggies for a salad? That's going to seriously screw with my vitamin intake." Duckie suppressed a chuckle at my quip, but Mom's sharp glance silenced him.

"That's not funny. It's important, Brooke. We want

to keep you safe, so there are rules you need to follow. For one"—she looked from me to Duckie—"straight to school and straight back. No stops along the way. Are you listening, Ronald?"

Swallowing a mouthful of breakfast, he nodded and said, "Yes, ma'am."

She placed a napkin beside my plate, as if this were any other day. But it wasn't. And we all knew it. As she took my phone from her pocket and set it in front of me, she said, "And if you don't answer right away when your father or I text or call you, we'll come looking for you."

I shook my head. Out of the corner of my eye, I saw something pink and then remembered that it was my hair. Funny the things you can forget when you're in the midst of getting seriously pissed off. "That's insane. What is this? Alcatraz?"

"This is serious." She gave me one last this-is-the-end-of-this-conversation look and then turned to rinse off the breakfast pans.

It was crazy. But when you've just been released from a mental hospital, people don't put much stock in what you think is crazy or not.

Duckie ate in silence for a bit, as if he was waiting for the storm to pass. Once Mom had finished cleaning up, she turned back to us and smiled cheerfully. "Now, I have to get the towels out of the dryer. You two enjoy catching up."

I didn't say anything in response. Not after she'd just told me I'd be under constant surveillance in my own home. Besides, there was a reason I'd told her yesterday that I didn't want to see Duckie. It wasn't because I was mad at him or anything. It was because I wanted to be alone. Because if anybody would be hurt by what I'd done, it would be Duckie, and I didn't want to see that hurt in his eyes when I looked at him. I couldn't deal with it, and she'd just flat-out ignored me. He was here now, eating breakfast in my kitchen, like today was any other day. I didn't know what to say to him.

But Duckie knew what to say. He always had. "I know you didn't want to see me yet. But I had to pull a friendship card and show up anyway. Because I missed you. And if that makes me selfish and makes you hate me, then so be it. I just needed to see your face."

I stared at my plate, not hungry at all.

"And your hair, apparently. Pink?" Duckie raised a sharp eyebrow. He knew me too well. "You hate pink."

I picked up the fork beside my plate and poked at the scrambled eggs. My throat felt dry, but I wasn't sure why. "I wanted something completely different. Something absolutely not me."

"Me too. Which is why I'm switching to dating girls." He paused, and I looked at him. After a moment, he waggled his eyebrows, cracking my stony exterior in the way that only Duckie could.

I laughed—a false laugh, one that felt brittle and too forced to be believed—and shoved his shoulder gently. "You are ridiculous."

"And your best friend. So if you think you can get rid of me, you're wrong. Just suck on that, lady." His tone was joking, but a hint of no-nonsense lurked beneath. I didn't want it to be there, that almost parental tone. I wanted Duckie to pretend with me for a little while that nothing had ever happened—that I hadn't tried to take my own life. That the worst things in front of us were pop quizzes and unrequited crushes.

Attempting to keep things light, I said, "That's what he said."

"Now who's being ridiculous?" He scooped up a forkful of eggs and smiled at me. There was no hesitation in his gaze, no expectation. Just that same adoring friendship that had always been there. "I-L-Y, Brooke."

We never said the actual words. We never told each other "I love you." Something about the words themselves would make it feel icky and strange. But we'd been saying those letters to each other since the third grade.

I smiled again, and this time I meant it. "I-L-Y too, Duckie."

Duckie chowed down on his food for a bit. I mostly moved mine around on my plate. Every once in a while, I'd jab a bit of scrambled egg and stick it in my mouth. I wasn't hungry at all, but I also didn't want to pass out from low blood sugar. Duckie wiped his mouth on his napkin and spoke without looking at me. His tone was careful and quiet, as if he understood that I was much like an animal in the wild now—skittish and afraid. He said, "We don't have to talk about it, okay? What happened. Not unless you want to. I just have to ask you one thing."

"What's that?" Every muscle in my body tightened. I didn't want to talk about what I'd failed to do, or why I'd tried to do it in the first place. I didn't want to talk about the stupid pills I had to take now, or the fact that every smile I attempted resembled a lopsided painting hanging on the wall. Much like before the moment I jumped, I wanted it all to go away. Everything. Forever.

But that was going to be so much harder since my parents had been appointed as my personal prison guards. Seriously, who locked away kitchen knives? Were the scissors hidden too? It'd be tough going, but they could work in a pinch.

Like always, Duckie seemed to know when to toe the line and when to cross it. Switching gears, he said, "Are you gonna eat that bacon, or . . . ?"

It was sweet the way he looked after me. The way he didn't want to hurt me any more than I was already hurting. But we both knew that conversation was coming, and that it would be coming soon.

Just not today, Duckie. Not today.

I nudged him with my elbow again. "I thought you were watching your girlish figure."

Rolling his eyes, he stole my remaining slice of bacon and shook it at me in a chastising way. "Honey, you've been gone six weeks. That diet has passed. Back to bacon and real life. Speaking of real life . . . when are you coming back to school? Your mom seems to think you need a week at home first."

I took a sip of orange juice. I was hoping it would be sweet, but it tasted sour. Bitter, even. "I'm going back tomorrow."

"You should probably tell her that." He gave me a side-long look. "Why the rush?"

I shrugged as nonchalantly as I could manage. "Like you said . . . back to bacon and real life."

"At times they are one and the same, my friend. One and the same." A good, honest laugh escaped me. Duckie was so absurd. He had a way of making sense of the senseless and the exact opposite too. There was little wonder why we were friends.

"It's good to hear you laugh. Maybe the medication is

working after all, eh?" My mom walked back into the room with the exact wrong thing to say. It was almost like feeling clouds roll in before a storm. My laughter stopped immediately, caught in my throat, almost choking me.

If only.

I wanted to tell her that depression doesn't work that way. That just because you have a moment of laughter and smiles and fun doesn't mean that you're not depressed. But I didn't say anything. Instead, I thought about scissors and X-Acto knives, and how accessible such things would be at school.

CHAPTER THREE

Whoever decided that teenagers should have to function and focus on math and grammar so early in the morning was clearly a sadist. My morning routine was brutal and took longer than I remembered, but after I showered, I dressed in two layered skirts that just barely reached my knee-high socks. I wore a baggy button-down shirt covered by a baggier cardigan sweater and fingerless gloves. The outfit was meant to cover my scars—which it did, quite successfully. The color palette was meant to blend in with the walls. Cream and various shades of gray. If I was lucky, no one at school would really notice me.

Duckie pulled into the driveway at 6:45, but I heard him coming from at least a mile away. His car, the mish-mashed antique pile of rust we affectionately referred to as the Beast, was a 1973 Volkswagen Beetle. Where it wasn't rusted, it was yellow, and the interior had been covered in green faux fur that reminded me of the Muppet monsters. It had a radio, but it only got two stations on AM and would only play cassettes. The backseat was missing half its cover-ing, so whenever anybody sat on that side, they were sitting on bare foam. The Beast also had two distinct smells: Fritos or whatever air freshener Duckie remembered to bring. It was a horrible car: it guzzled gas like a man stumbling out of the desert might guzzle water, and every time Duckie put it in park, it would backfire loudly.

Naturally, it was Duckie's prized possession, and we both loved it dearly.

I opened the passenger-side door and slid into the Beast, relieved that Duckie had remembered some air freshener. He smiled at me as I closed the door and put on my seat belt. "You ready for this?"

I wasn't, and I wouldn't lie to Duckie about that. I wasn't ready to walk into a high school I'd thought I'd left forever. I shook my head at him and slid down some in my seat. Duckie didn't say anything in response. He just looked at me all concerned and put the Beast in drive. We didn't talk during our ten-minute commute. Mostly because I didn't know what to say. I was relieved that Duckie didn't say anything more either. I didn't want to be caught up on the latest gossip or pretend that this was a normal day. I just wanted to get through it and get home. Like ripping a Band-Aid off.

Duckie parked as close to the school as he could, which was very different from his usual spot. Normally, he'd park in the back of the lot so we could take our time getting to the building and facing all the crap that came with being in high school. When I threw a questioning glance his way, he said, "In case you need a quick getaway."

His words lifted the corner of my mouth in a hint of a smile. So much for his pledge to bring me straight to school and straight home afterward. Duckie was probably the best friend that anyone could ask for. He got it. He got me. Without me having to say a word, he knew how I was feeling. And he'd always been that way with me. I wondered if he'd suspected my intentions before I went to Black River, or if he suspected them now. I hoped not. Better that he not know. But if anyone could read my mind, it was Duckie. It was probably the most frustrating thing about being friends with him.

We'd arrived well after the buses, which meant fewer people in the parking lot or milling about outside. Once we stepped inside, it was another story entirely. Students, teachers, tons of the usual people were everywhere I looked. And it felt like all eyes were on me with each step I took down the hall.

Familiar faces seemed strange to me, as if I were looking at old photographs instead of living in the moment. Penny Curtis, Steve Hillard, Quentin Daly—all kids I knew. All friends I'd regularly hung out with. These were people who'd helped me decorate the gym for school dances, who'd pulled pranks on substitute teachers with me just for kicks. I'd known them all since I was in pigtails and sundresses. But they looked at me now like I was an apparition of some sort, something not quite tangible. I was a stranger to them. A ghost. How fitting.

Duckie pretended not to notice the stares, but that didn't make them any less real. He pulled open the door to the main office, and we went inside. Mrs. Kellog was sitting behind the front desk, glasses perched on the end of her nose, her favorite ugly, ruffled flower shirt still as ruffled and ugly and flower-covered as I remembered. I cleared my throat to get her attention, and when she looked at me, I said, "Hi. I'm returning to class today after an extended absence. I believe my mom sent an email . . . ?"

With a heavy I-hate-my-job sigh, she slapped a pink piece of paper on the receptionist's desk beside the chained-down pen. She looked at me over the rims of her glasses.

"What's the reason for your absence?"

"Medical." I'd practiced the word in my head all morning. While brushing my teeth. While taking small bites of my ham-and-cheese omelet. While swallowing the pills that Dr. Canton had prescribed to me at Kingsdale.

The look in her eyes said she knew very well what the reason was for my absence. The question of how that could be entered my thoughts, but was replaced with relief when she took the paper back and sighed. "You'll need to see your guidance counselor before I can let you return to class."

Of course. Because bureaucracy was way more important than devoting time to one's education. Fine. Whatever. They could say it was school policy for a student to meet with the school counselor before returning to class, that they wanted to make certain the student was prepared and informed about what had transpired in their absence. But I had my own suspicions as to why Mr. Clemons wanted to see me. Simply put, he was nosy and wanted as much dirt on what had happened as he could dig up. Something interesting to chat about over bad coffee in the teachers' lounge.

Nodding, I said, "Okay. When can I do that?"

"Have a seat. I'll let him know you're here." She flicked a glare at Duckie. "Ronald, you should get to class."

"I just wanted to wait for Brooke."

"Class. Now. Or I'll write you up."

Duckie turned toward the door, but not before engaging me in silent conversation with our eyes. He said, *What a bitch.*

I said, *Mega bitch. Wait for me outside?*

He said, *You know I will. I-L-Y.*

I said, *I-L-Y too.*

While I waited, I pulled some paper out of my backpack and folded several origami cranes. They didn't make me feel any better or impose upon me this amazing will to live or anything. But they gave me something to do while I thought about my plan. It was just a matter of deciding on a method and an instrument, picking a time when I was certain I'd be alone, and doing it. I placed the paper cranes inside my bag. They looked up at me in approval.

Random teachers and students wandered in and out of the office for several minutes. The first bell rang through the halls, and the shuffle of feet followed. Was anyone ever on time to the first class of the day? I doubted it.

Across from me sat Sarah Emberson, a pretty girl with freckles, big blue eyes, and rainbow-dyed hair. She was doing her best not to meet my eyes. I had a feeling she was still embarrassed about asking me out during the first week of school. I was totally flattered and thanked her before informing her that I just wasn't into girls. I thought I'd handled it okay, but she'd run into the girls' room crying and wouldn't talk to me after that.

When she finally dared a glance at me, I said, "Hey, Sarah."

She ripped her gaze away, and I had a feeling that would be the extent of our interaction while we sat in the office waiting area. After a while, my phone buzzed inside my sweater pocket, breaking the tension a bit. It was Duckie. I knew it was him before I even looked at the screen. Because it always was. He texted me more than anyone, and at any time, day or night. It was just his way. I pulled it out and read the text. **Just got yelled at by Miller, so I can't wait for you. See you in class, k?**

Miller was our school resource officer. Not that our school really had any need for a security guard. But with so many school shootings in the news, the PTA had insisted and the school board had agreed, and now we were stuck with an overly enthusiastic mall cop in charge of our safety. He carried a Taser on his hip and looked like he used steroids and spent way too much time at the gym. We were still trying to figure out why he chose to work at a high school, considering how much he seemed to loathe teenagers. Duckie's theory was that he was probably some psycho who tortured puppies in his spare time. Mine centered more around the idea that maybe he had been made to feel powerless by someone when he was in high school, so this was his way of getting back at them and righting the wrongs of his past. But either way you swung it, Miller was a dick.

"Brooke Danvers?" Mr. Clemons came out of his office. The top of his head was bald, but the rest of his head was clinging to the wisps of graying hair around the sides. He was shorter than me, and I'd only spoken to him three times throughout my entire high school existence—at the end of each year, when I was finalizing my class schedule for the following school year. I was hoping our little pow-wow wouldn't take long. I wanted to just begin the school day already so that it could end and I could go home.

I stepped inside his office, and he closed the door behind us before taking a seat at his desk and shuffling some papers around. As I sat in one of the round chairs in front of him, I realized that his office smelled a bit like cinnamon rolls. My stomach rumbled. Maybe I should have eaten more at breakfast. I was mostly just feeling nauseous at the idea of coming back to school. But I'd taken my meds. Mom might let me get out the door without downing a huge breakfast, but she was damn sure going to make me swallow those pills.

Mr. Clemons leaned over his desk on his forearms, folding his fingers together neatly. He tilted his head and opened his eyes just a bit wider. This was what I called the how-are-you pose. It was inevitably followed by "How are you, Brooke? I mean, since your little accident."

I bristled. A. It hadn't been an accident. B. Clearly my mother had told the school about my suicide attempt, which was just *awesome*. And 3. I was fairly sure that Mr. Clemons didn't really give a crap about how I was. I didn't take well to gossips like him, and I sure as hell wasn't about to update my high school counselor on the reality of my mental health situation. So I opened my mouth and lied. I was getting good at it. Not that he was deserving of anything intricate. Just a simple lie. Just enough to let him know that I was done with this line of conversation and that it was none of his business. "I'm fine."

He nodded slowly, disappointment filling his expression. I guess he'd have to chitchat about local news and sports in the lounge this afternoon. "I see. Well, I'm glad to hear it. Are you on any medications that I should be aware of?"

"As I don't take any medication during school hours . . . No. None that you should be aware of."

The corner of his mouth twitched and he nodded slowly, formulating the words in his mind before unleashing the Dr. Phil–ness into the world. "Your parents have sent along a letter stating that you should be kept from sharp objects and the like. I thought you should be made aware that we here at Eleos High have nothing but your best interests and safety in mind, so we'll make certain that such . . . such . . . uhh . . . temptations . . . remain out of reach as best as we are able to."

Great. Just what I needed. Twenty-four-hour surveillance.

The paper cranes shifted around uncomfortably. Pills were out. Sharp objects were out. We were being watched and needed a new plan. Fast.

Mr. Clemons lowered his voice, despite the fact that the door was closed and no one else could hear. "I just wanted to let you know that I'm available to talk. About anything that might be troubling you. I wanted to reach out and tell you that I care, and I'm here for you if you need me."

Angry breath caught in my throat, burning its way down into my chest. He had a lot of nerve saying so, when we both knew he was full of it. "Really?"

He nodded again, leaning forward and looking at me with doe eyes. This was his chance. Get all the dirty details and be the popular guy at the gossip table. My guess was that Mr. Clemons had certainly not been the popular guy in his high school days. The eagerness emanating from him was making me even more nauseous. "Absolutely."

I clenched my jaw and glanced at the poster that was hanging on the wall behind his desk. It featured an enormous image of a rainbow and the phrase "Minds are like parachutes—they work best when open." When I looked back at Mr. Clemons, my left eye twitched. I said, "If you cared so much about me, then where were you when things were falling apart? Why didn't you notice? Why didn't you help me?"

Not that I'd wanted his help, but if he was going to sit here now and pretend to give a single fuck about me, I was going to lay it on thick and call him out on his bullshit. Not today, Dr. Phil. Not today.

His doe eyes suddenly widened as my accusing headlights reached him. "I . . ."

His words trailed off, and I stood and slung my backpack over my shoulder. "You don't care. You don't even know me, apart from what classes I'm taking. You're just nosy. So if you don't mind, I'm going to class now."

Mr. Clemons took his time pulling the small pad of yellow paper closer to him. As he scribbled his signature on the hall pass for me, he said, "You're wrong, Brooke. I do care. Everyone who knows you cares."

"That explains all the cards and flowers I received at the hospital." I snatched the paper from his outstretched hand. "FYI, I got one card and one bouquet of flowers. The flowers were from my parents. And the card was from Duckie. So the rest of you can kiss my—"

"Brooke."

It was stupid, this discussion. Stupid and utterly pointless. What I'd done wasn't about getting attention or making people notice me. It wasn't a plea for help or an exclamation of my inner pain. It was about erasing myself from existence. It was about ending my pain altogether. I was sick of myself, sick of my life, sick of everything and everyone around me. I was tired. Tired of trying to fit in. Tired of living. Only I couldn't even get suicide right. And nobody cared that I was still alive. Oh, they would have wept at my funeral, I'm sure. People like Claire, the head cheerleader, would have hugged people like David, president of the anime club, and cried together over my open casket. For a few hours, there would be no divisions between the kids with money and the kids without. For a few hours, popularity wouldn't matter and people would say things like "She was so young" and "I just don't understand." For a few hours, the world would seem to change in the light of such a tragedy. But it would be back to business the following school day. Because death changes nothing—it just makes people scared of their own eventuality.

I knew, because I'd been to two funerals for kids I went to school with. And each experience was an exact replica of the other. Those kids lived and died, and all they had to show for it was a page in the yearbook. But at least they didn't have to put up with the bullshit anymore.

As I walked out of the office with that yellow slip of paper in my hand, the cranes flipped Mr. Clemons off, and when we passed the front desk, they flipped Mrs. Kellog off too for good measure.

I moved down the empty hall, past the green-gray lockers to room 131. As I reached out to open the door, I felt my breath lock inside my lungs. There was no turning back now.

Suddenly I was standing on the edge of the stone bridge in the middle of the night. The water below rushed under the bridge, beckoning to me. I leaned forward past my tipping point, and right before my feet left the ground, I thought, *There's no turning back now.*

I opened the door. Ms. Naples stopped midsentence as she looked up at me. All eyes were on me as I moved forward and gave her the hall pass in my hand. Someone in the back of the class cleared their throat, but that was the only sound besides the increased beating of my heart. Ms. Naples flashed me that concerned look that I'd been expecting to find on her face. I was sure I'd see it at least once a class today. Seven classes. Seven teachers. Seven concerned expressions. It was enough to make me long for that quick escape that Duckie had mentioned earlier. She took my hall pass and whispered, "Welcome back, Brooke."

As usual, Duckie was sitting in the back of the room.

There was an empty desk right beside his, and I was grateful he'd saved me a seat. At least he wouldn't push me to talk about the river or why I'd done it or ask me ridiculous questions about how I was feeling. Not yet, anyway. I moved to the back of the class and Ms. Naples picked up where she'd left off, rambling on about the importance of economics or some such crap. As I took my seat, I dropped my backpack on the floor beside me.

Quentin was sitting to my left. I gave him a little wave, but he squirmed uncomfortably in his seat. I wondered how long it took for gossip to flow from the head office, all the way through the halls, permeating an entire school. Did Quentin know about my attempt? Did everyone?

Duckie leaned over and whispered, "I sure hope you plan on taking notes, because I am so over this crap, it's ridiculous."

Ever his hero in economics, I pulled out a notebook and scribbled down what sounded like test-worthy information. It was cool, though. I'd always saved him in any class that was even close to being math related, and he rescued me in all the sciences. We both had a strong grasp of all things word related, so we never really worried about that.

About midway through class, Ms. Naples started helping a few students with questions they had. Duckie had fallen asleep at his desk, a thin line of drool connecting his face to the books he was lying on. I made paper cranes and stared at the clock, willing it to move faster. When the bell rang at the end of class, I nudged Duckie awake and stuffed the new cranes in with the ones I'd made in the office. I imagined them nodding to one another in greeting, maybe shaking the tips of their wings together like tiny hands. They didn't have names. They didn't need names. The cranes were me, and I was them.

Once in the hall, Duckie and I pushed our way through the crowd like salmon swimming upstream, all the way to our lockers, which were somehow, blissfully, right next to each other this year. On the door of my locker, someone had written "RIP" in big, black letters with a Sharpie.

At first I didn't really get why it was there—maybe someone had heard about my attempt and thought that I'd succeeded. Maybe I had died after all and high school was my eternal hell—if there was such a thing.

After a few moments of contemplation, I realized what the vandal had meant. They hadn't meant "Rest in Peace." They'd meant "We know, Brooke. We know you tried to kill yourself, and rather than give you reasons not to, we're punishing you for having failed. Maybe we thought you were normal before, but now we all know what a freak you are, and we will never, ever let you forget it."

It should have hurt, I suppose. But really, I was numb to

it. It didn't matter. I was just a ghost to them now. Despite breathing, walking, and talking—despite my heart beating in my chest—I was already dead.

Duckie's face flushed red with anger. He muttered, "Don't worry about it. I'll tell the janitor and he'll have it scrubbed away or painted over before the day is out."

For some reason, he was good friends with all the janitors at Eleos High. Just as he'd been friends with the janitors in our middle school, and in elementary. I'd asked him once why he went out of his way to get to know them and he'd told me that they were some of the nicest people he'd ever met. He hated the way some of the kids looked down on them just because their job involved a mop and broom. Duckie was the kindest person I knew.

I stared at the thick, black letters on my locker, which had been very carefully written. Whoever wrote them took their time doing so. They wanted to drive that message home, for sure. Across the hall, Sarah Emberson and her girlfriend, Kristah Neil, were standing there exchanging whispers and gesturing to my locker. They weren't alone. Several students had noticed the graffiti, and so had one of the office ladies who only filled in whenever somebody was sick. Maybe whoever did it was also watching now, waiting for tears to well up in my eyes and for me to run down the hall in pain. But I was beyond that sort of pain now. "It doesn't matter, Duckie. They'll just do it again anyway."

Duckie leaned against the lockers and brushed a pink strand from my eyes. "It does matter. Because you're a person, not a headline . . . or a punch line."

I met his eyes, and for a moment, I wanted to apologize for what I'd put him through, what I was about to put him through. But then I looked away. For some things there were no words. Besides, no one could know that suicidal plans were still brewing inside of me. Because if someone had even a hint of an idea that I was going to try again, my plan would fail. And I wanted to get it right this time.

I just had to figure out how.

Turning the dial on my locker, I was somewhat surprised that I remembered how to open it after a month and a half away. It felt like I hadn't been to school in a million years, in another lifetime, on another plane of existence. But there it was, my combination, as if it had been engraved on my brainstem: 24-6-12.

I opened the door and exchanged my economics book for government and a copy of *Twelfth Night*. I wouldn't see Duckie again until lunch after third period, and I was dreading facing two classes without him. Duckie must have been feeling the same way, because as he opened his locker to get his books, he sighed. "Maybe we should just volunteer with Ms.

Quinn the rest of the day. I'm sure she'll give us a pass, and she is in the middle of reorganizing the entire library."

From inside my backpack, the paper cranes gave me a collective, reassuring nod. I shook my head at Duckie and said, "I'll keep it in mind, but let's not seek asylum there just yet. Maybe later."

He hooked his right pinkie with mine and shook it, just like we used to do in middle school whenever we made promises to each other. "See you at lunch. Don't take any crap."

I moved down the hall to Mr. Rober's government class. The chairs were all in a semicircle, because Mr. Rober said it was an equalizer. Ironic that a man who frequently talked down to women would think his students needed equalization. But whatever. I took the seat nearest the door, just in case I needed a quick escape. For a moment, I lost myself in a fantasy in which I bolted from the room, impossibly back-flipped all the way down the hall, and ran out the door to the Beast, where Duckie was waiting. We peeled out in a haze of exhaust and burnt tires and left the school behind forever. In my head, Alice Cooper's "School's Out" played as we made our dramatic exit.

Students filed in, including Penny Curtis and Steve Hillard. I looked at them as they entered, but rather than sit near me, they moved quickly across the room and took their seats there. My heart sank a little. Apparently word had traveled fast.

Unfortunately for Claire Simpson, there were no other chairs left open but the one to my left. She sighed heavily as she took her seat. I laid my head on my desk, using my folded arms as a pillow, willing the class to pass quickly. I didn't mean to fall asleep, but the next thing I knew, the bell rang, signifying the end of class. I sat up, wiping the drool from the corner of my mouth with the back of my hand and hating Mr. Rober even more for having let me sleep the whole time, where everyone could see. But then, I went out of my way to find reasons to hate Mr. Rober. The guy was a jerk.

As if sensing my hatred, Mr. Rober said, "Miss Danvers. A moment, if you will."

Begrudgingly, I picked up my backpack and walked over to his desk. "Yeah?"

His eyebrows were so thick and twisted that they looked like two very angry caterpillars had taken residence on his face. When he raised them, the caterpillars looked even angrier. "Here is the packet of classwork and homework that you missed during your absence. I expect it completed within two weeks."

He handed me a stack of papers and I stuffed them inside my bag. Two weeks. Right. That was totally going to happen.

(Insert sarcasm here.) "Okay."

Once I left Mr. Rober and his angry caterpillars behind, I moved down the hall, ignoring the whispers and stares. Most came from the kids in Mr. Rober's class, but too many didn't. Let them talk. Let them gossip. Let them judge. It made no difference.

My next class was a Shakespeare elective with Mrs. Carnes. She was a nice-enough teacher, so I wasn't dreading her class too much. She didn't put up with rudeness and insisted that everyone only engage in class discussions if we were comfortable. I moved to the back of the room and sat, waiting for class to begin and finish as quickly as possible. The bell rang again and Mrs. Carnes walked in, dressed in a pretty yellow dress that swished around her calves when she turned. "Good morning, everyone."

Several people returned her greeting. Most just sat and stared at the front of the room, likely willing the school day to hurry up and end already. I was right there with them.

Mrs. Carnes looked at me and smiled gently. "Brooke, could I see you up here for a minute, please?"

All eyes were on me as I approached her desk. I didn't see them, but I could sense them.

"I didn't get a chance to swing by during visitors' hours, but Karen and I got you a gift to wish you well on your recovery. I hope you don't mind." Karen was Mrs. Carnes's wife.

Everybody in the school knew and most people didn't care. I'd once met Karen at the mall. She looked like Mrs. Carnes's polar opposite: tall, tan, short hair. But they were a nice couple. When they got married a few months ago, Duckie and I gave them a congratulations card. Them getting me a gift was thoughtful, and I appreciated it before I even knew what it was. She handed me a journal that looked like an old suitcase covered in travel labels on the outside.

I smiled and said, "Thank you. And thank Karen for me too."

The air felt a tad lighter as I returned to my desk, but any lightness that I felt was erased the moment I spied the new graffiti that had been written on my notebook while I'd been at the front of the room. In bold, black Sharpie, it read "RIP."

I stared at it a moment before taking my seat again, wondering which one of these assholes was responsible for it. Was it the same person who'd written it on my locker? The rest of the class blurred into the background, with only one point of clarity—the graffiti on my notebook.

They would never let me forget. But the joke was on them, because cruel pranks—as far as I knew—didn't follow you into oblivion. I was untouchable.

After the bell rang, I shoved my stuff inside my backpack. The cranes scurried away from the notebook, not wanting to go anywhere near it. I couldn't blame them.

Duckie was waiting for me outside the lunchroom. I decided not to tell him about the new graffiti. He'd just want to fix it by hunting down whoever did it and turning them in. But that wouldn't help. It couldn't be helped.

After I stepped up to him, I straightened his bow tie. "You're crooked."

The corner of his mouth tugged up in a small smirk. "Well, I'm certainly not straight."

I smoothed out the fabric of his bow tie with my fingers, marveling at Duckie's original sense of style. I always aimed for comfort. He always aimed for unique. "You hungry?"

"Extremely. A shame we have to eat here. I don't care what the cafeteria lady says. Whatever they're serving on trays in the cafeteria doesn't qualify as food." As we made our way to our usual table, he said, "How's today been so far?"

I could hear the whispers around us and wondered if they were about me. Maybe I was just being paranoid. And even if they were gossiping about me, what difference did it make to tell them to stop? People would talk. It's what people did.

I dropped my backpack on the floor beside the table and sank into my seat, shrugging and wondering if my dad had anything in the garage that would serve my life-ending purposes. Had they been that thorough? "Kinda quiet, I guess. Better than I expected."

Duckie gauged my eyes for several seconds, as if reading me, looking closely for any sign that I might not be telling the truth. After a moment, he said, "Wait here. I'll grab your food. You save my spot."

He wedged his way into the middle of the lunch line. If it had been anyone but Tucker standing there, he wouldn't have had a chance at cutting in. But I had a feeling that Tucker was as into Duckie as Duckie was into him. If only Duckie could see it. But then, Duckie was a gay boy in a small town. His options here were limited, and his experiences had made him more than a little gun shy.

I wanted Duckie to find happiness. No. I *needed* him to. Because I was never getting out of this darkness, and I just had to know that when it was over, when I was gone, at least one of us would find a life worth living.

I swept my eyes across the lunchroom, feeling like an alien who'd only just recently landed here on Earth. As usual, Jake Taylor was entertaining the other kids on the robotics team with jokes about sex—not that he had any personal experience in that department, from what I'd heard. Sarah Emberson and Kristah Neil were tossing french fries from where they sat over at quiet, mousy, not-always-clean Milly Sims, who was too immersed in her paperback to even notice. Sarah glanced my way and declared a cease-fire as she whispered something into Kristah's ear, eliciting a burst of laughter. Scott Melbur was wandering the cafeteria with his camera, snapping random photos for the yearbook. It was nice to see the once most-reviled person in our entire school find his niche and stop being the butt of nearly everyone's jokes. Various cliques gathered together at separate tables, and those who weren't in any particular clique filled in the blanks of the room. For the moment, it was business as usual at Eleos High. All around me was a sea of familiar faces . . . but for one.

He wore blue-black jeans and a faded gray V-neck T-shirt. The short chain around his neck was dull silver, and the heavy black boots on his feet said he rode a motorcycle. Or at least that he looked like he did. His eyes were aqua blue and reminded me of the pictures my mom and dad had brought back from their vacation to the Caribbean last fall. His eyes were like the ocean. Warm, but cool. Dangerous, but appealing. I found it difficult not to look at them. At him.

His hair was dirty blond and disheveled, but short. There was a slight natural curl to it, and I couldn't help but think what it might feel like to run my fingers through it.

As the thought passed through my mind, he lifted his gaze to mine. Our eyes met, and I wondered if he could tell by my expression what I had been thinking about him.

Maybe I should have smiled at him, or nodded, or waved

like a normal person. But instead, I just stared at him awkwardly until he looked away again. I couldn't help it. It just kind of happened that way. Not that it mattered. Nothing mattered now but my plan and the fact that my time here was ticking away.

"It's green." Duckie set his tray beside mine and sighed in exasperation.

What he was referring to, of course, was the weird rectangular cut of pizza that sat on each of our lunch trays. I looked at it and shrugged. "It's always green. Maybe they grind up broccoli or kale or something and mix it with the cheese in an effort to force us into a healthier diet."

Duckie rolled his eyes and reached for a reliable french fry. "Puh-lease. It's mold. This pizza is older than me."

I cracked open my tiny pint carton of chocolate milk and took a swig, flicking my eyes toward the newcomer and trying hard to sound blasé. "Who's he, anyway?"

Duckie glanced over his shoulder at the boy in the biker boots. When he turned back to me, a playful smile was dancing on his lips. "Why do you wanna know?"

Why did I want to know? Maybe because he seemed interesting. Or maybe it was because of the way my chest had tightened slightly at the sight of him. But I wouldn't say. Not even to Duckie. "I just wanna know, okay?"

Duckie's left eyebrow was raised sharply. He didn't believe me. Not even one bit. "Just curious, eh? Nothing to do with the fact that he's rock 'n' roll gorgeous?"

"Duckie," I pleaded, hoping he wouldn't push me today.

After a moment, Duckie sighed. "He moved here about three weeks ago. His name is Derek Holloway. He's a senior. And he is straight."

It was my turn to raise an eyebrow. My eyes drifted back to Derek before returning to Duckie. "How can you tell?"

"I just can." He shrugged. "He's single too. You interested?"

Inside my backpack, the paper cranes whispered before shaking their tiny heads at me collectively. "I don't have time for a relationship."

Duckie reached out and cupped his hand over mine, giving it a gentle squeeze. As afraid as I was that he might see my intentions lurking in my eyes, I met his gaze. Duckie wasn't smiling. Duckie wasn't putting on his charm. Duckie was, in one of his rarer moments, being completely sincere. I both loved him and hated him for it. "Honey, you just went through hell. All you have is time right now. If you let yourself."

We sat there like that for a while, until I finally slipped my hand slowly out from under his. I picked up the apple from my lunch tray and stood, slinging my backpack over one shoulder. "Let's get out of here."

Duckie stood up without hesitation. "Where do you wanna go?"

I shook my head. I had no answers. "Anywhere. Just . . . away."

"Library?"

"Library." On our way out of the lunchroom, I set the apple I was holding on the table in front of the new guy. I wasn't sure why. Maybe I just wanted to show him that not everyone in the world is the kind of person to write "RIP" on someone's locker. Maybe I just felt like being nice to someone on a day when it felt like very few people had been nice to me.

He looked up at me, his ocean eyes rolling over me in waves. He opened his mouth to say something, but I turned and walked away before he had the chance.

As I exited the room with Duckie in tow, I let the new guy's name turn over gently in my mind. *Derek.*

What a nice name.

CHAPTER FOUR

As expected, Ms. Quinn was really overwhelmed and happy to have some help reorganizing the library that afternoon. While she filled out paperwork, Duckie and I got to work moving the chairs and tables around. She put us on shelf-moving duty after that—which sucked, but removing books and relocating the shelves before putting the books back in their rightful place seemed a hell of a lot better than facing the rest of the day's classes. Besides, since it was just we three, she let us put music on while we worked.

Ms. Quinn was, without doubt, the coolest person on staff at Eleas High. She didn't let anybody give anybody else any crap in her library. And if you needed a hall pass or a break from class for a good reason, she really understood.

"Hey, Brooke, would you mind clearing off the bulletin board and hanging up the papers in that stack on the counter? It looks like it's getting pretty crowded. I've gotta run these to the office real quick," she said, knowing I'd be fine with it, and stepped out the door with an armload of freshly printed fliers before I could answer.

The bulletin board was just inside the library doors, right next to the front desk. School clubs posted stuff there about meetings. School functions were advertised there. Anyone could use it, and they did.

Anyone. Including whoever had apparently posted a poorly designed invitation to my funeral.

I reached up to take it down, my chest heavy and hollow. But before the tips of my fingers could make contact with the page, Duckie ripped it from the board and said, "What the hell?! Who does shit like this?"

No words formed on my tongue. Because I was past wondering, past caring.

Duckie's face was flushed with anger. He shredded the invitation into bits and threw them on the ground before grabbing me by the arm. "Come on. I don't care what your mom and dad said. We're getting you out of here *now*."

I didn't argue. I just grabbed my backpack and followed.

Sneaking out of Eleos High wasn't exactly like breaking out of prison—even though it felt that way. Miller should have been keeping an eye on the front door, but as usual, he was hitting on the young blond office assistant whose name I could never remember. So while Miller was working on getting some, Duckie and I just slid out the front door and made our way to the Beast as quickly and as nonchalantly as we could. So much for school security.

But then, people were kidding themselves if they thought that resource officers were the answer to all the violence in schools. They were merely placeholders. They were there to make parents and the administration smile and nod and pat themselves on the back for doing something.

The fact was, no one really survived high school. Sure, most people live on after graduation—but something in them stays behind in its jaws. Like bits of meat trapped between the teeth of a hungry animal. I'd seen it in my dad's eyes whenever the subject turned to his days in school. High school took a bite out of your soul.

My seat belt was barely buckled when the Beast's engine sputtered to life. Dropping my backpack to the floor between my feet, I could tell the paper cranes inside were sighing in relief at granting ourselves an early dismissal. Duckie pulled out of the parking lot and headed west. I knew exactly where he was going without him having to say a word. We rolled the windows down, and the warm breeze blew through the car, knocking Duckie's fedora into the backseat and blowing my hair from my face. When we reached Washburn Road he turned left, taking us farther out into the country. On the corner was a sign that read "Spencer—6.5 miles." But we weren't going to Spencer. We were going to a place that I was pretty sure only Duckie and I ever visited—somewhere we could be alone.

Closing my eyes, I let myself enjoy the warmth of the sun on my face. Duckie popped a cassette into the tape deck. It didn't take long for me to recognize the song. It was "Lovesong" by The Cure. Duckie had discovered a shoe box full of cassettes in the trunk when he'd bought the Beast. Most were crap. But The Cure was definitely a keeper, and the tape was one we listened to often.

I let the music take me away for a while, losing myself in the light and sweetness of spring as Duckie drove us down a crumbling paved road and then turned onto a dirt one. He drove about a mile before he pulled into an overgrown, mostly forgotten parking lot connected to an old elementary school. Weeds had filled the cracks in the pavement, and rain and sun had washed and bleached away the painted lines. The building still stood, but most of the windows had been boarded up. The outside was home to spray-painted words. Apparently someone named Jesse had been here at one point—the graffiti said so in big, red letters—and I had a feeling I knew which Jesse it was. But the building didn't matter. It wasn't our destination. Where we were going was behind the old elementary school, to the place where Duckie and I first met.

The playground looked pretty much like it had back in kindergarten. Only there were more weeds now and the equipment was rusting away. At the center of the play-ground stood the massive metal climbing dome. Behind that were the teeter-totters and the basketball court. To the left were the swings and the slide that Duckie had fallen off in the third grade. He'd broken his arm and cried harder than I'd ever seen him cry before or since. I'd signed his cast "I-L-Y—B." Last I knew, he still had the cast.

Duckie sat on one of the swings and pushed back with his feet, swinging forward. The chains creaked under his weight, but held. He said, "Come on. Let's swing."

Doubtful about the equipment's ability to remain in one piece under the strain of two teenagers, I slowly sank into the swing beside him and looked at the back of the school. "Do you remember when they built the new elementary school on the other side of town? We were so mad. You staged a protest."

He smiled in remembrance. "I was a pissed-off fourth grader. You don't mess with routine at that age."

I offered a halfhearted shrug. "The new school wasn't so bad. I mean, it was okay."

"Not great, though. Not like this one." He was right, and we both knew it. The last time I could remember being truly happy was when we were attending this school, swinging on these swings, not caring about tomorrow or the years to come. All we had back in those days were songs by Queen, games of tag, and arguing over the last chocolate-peanut-butter treat in the cafeteria. Life was simple then. Just Pokémon, building forts, and wishing on stars.

I looked at the main building, at the boarded-up windows. Someone had spray-painted a Nazi symbol on one of the boards. What an asshole. "You were the best part of this school for me."

The wind blew gently, and a large, white cloud moved overhead, casting a shadow on us before moving along and leaving us in the sunshine again.

"Can I ask you something?" Duckie wasn't swinging anymore. Nor was he looking at me. I knew what he was going to ask before he even opened his mouth again. I wished he wouldn't. "Why'd you do it?"

It. The word was so much easier to say than asking me why I'd attempted suicide. But I understood. Just the word *suicide* made people uncomfortable. Hell, it made me uncomfortable—but I'd rather people just ask me outright than pussyfoot around it.

I drew a heart in the dirt with the toe of my shoe, then stomped on it, leaving an imprint of my sneaker in the middle. If I didn't answer him, he'd just keep asking. That was always his way. So I took a slow breath into my lungs and said, "I can't tell you why. Because you wouldn't understand. It's not any one thing. It's just . . . everything."

I could feel him looking at me, willing me to meet his gaze. But I refused, instead focusing on all the weeds that had grown up around the playground. How did such an awesome place become so used up and worn out? "You're speaking in present tense. Do I have to worry you'll do it again?"

I pushed back with my feet and lifted them up, letting myself swing back and forth for a minute.

Finally Duckie grabbed one of the chains of my swing and stopped me. "Brooke. Seriously."

I stared forward, my eyes locked on that stupid Nazi graffiti. For a moment, I felt more robotic than human. "No. You don't have anything to worry about."

He didn't believe me, and I was waiting for him to call me on it. We both knew that killing myself was still very much on my mind. But I'd deny it to the very end. I think we both knew that too.

To my amazement, he dropped the subject without so much as an argument. For the moment, at least. "Prom's coming up. You going with me or what?"

"That's a hell of a way to ask someone to be your date to prom. Some people propose such a thing in grand gestures that make the askee swoon. I get asked on a decrepit swing set with 'or what?' attached." I nudged him with my elbow, but he didn't smile. So I tried a different approach. "I thought you were going to ask Tucker."

His eyes lit up at the mere mention of Tucker. "And risk having my heart broken by a pretty boy with brown eyes and a dashing smile? Nah. I'd rather go with you."

"Liar."

"That makes two of us, doesn't it?" Suddenly the lightness of the moment was gone. Duckie was done with casual conversation. He was done pretending that everything was roses and rainbows with me, the way my mother had pretended on the drive home from Kingsdale. He was ready to talk about what I had done that night at Black River, whether I was ready to or not. "Look. I know you don't want to hear it, but you scared the shit out of me, and I'm worried about you. Since your mom's phone call from the hospital, I've been going over all sorts of things you said or did in the past, looking back to see if there were any signs you were that close to the edge. Then I remembered the bandages on your arm. You were cutting, weren't you? Just tell me."

My jaw tightened stubbornly. "Take me home now."

"Not until you tell me what really happened. I wanna hear it from you, Brooke. Not from whispers in the hall. Not from carefully worded medical descriptions. I want to hear what exactly you were thinking, feeling, doing that night. From you. My best friend."

"Fine. I'll walk." I stood up, and he immediately caught my hand in his.

"I'm sorry. I just . . . I can't pretend that it didn't happen." He wouldn't have to, but he had no way of knowing that. "Come on. Stay. We can still have fun."

But the fun was over. The stolen moment of peace and reminiscence had been tainted. "Just take me home."

The drive back to my house was long and silent. And when we finally pulled into my driveway, I got out with my backpack and shut the door hard behind me. Duckie didn't say a word, but I could feel his apology hanging in the air. I moved up the walk and let myself in without looking back at him.

I arrived home an hour earlier than I would have if I'd stayed at school the entire day. No one else should have been home, but as I started heading up the stairs, my dad cleared his throat to get my attention. He and Mom were sitting in the living room, waiting for me. That was never a good sign.

Dad pointed to the couch, and I begrudgingly took a seat but said nothing.

Mom began. "The school called today."

Shit.

"They said you missed your last two classes and that you were seen leaving school grounds in Ronald's car." Her mouth was a thin, angry line. "What do you have to say for yourself?"

"Nothing, I guess. But it was my idea. I had to practically threaten Duckie to get him to come with me." The lie left my mouth easily, and with good reason. If they had any clue that skipping school had been Duckie's idea, I'd be grounded from seeing him until the end of time.

Dad muttered, "At least one of you has some semblance of good sense."

"You know the rules. Straight to school and straight back. *No* stops." Mom was raising her voice, but I wasn't sure she was aware of it.

In direct contrast, Dad's voice was calm. Too calm. Scary calm. "Perhaps taking the bus is a better idea for you."

Spit wads, dick jokes, and the rampant smell of body odor hit my memory like a Mack truck. Was he serious?

"Dad, I'm a senior. Do you have any idea how ridiculous

I'd look riding with the lowerclassmen?"

"We could always hire a tutor and have you home-schooled." He leaned forward in his seat, eyes on me. He was challenging me. Warning me. The room suddenly felt much warmer than it had earlier. Uncomfortably so. "You tell us, then. What other option is there? Because today you proved that we can't trust you."

"I'm sorry, okay? We just went out to our old elementary school and sat on the swings for a while. Duckie asked me to prom. It was really no big deal. He was with me the entire time." I flicked my eyes between them, wanting more than anything for them to believe me.

My mother snapped, "If you're lying to us—"

"I'm not. Really. It won't happen again." It was another lie, but the truth was going to get me precisely nowhere.

A long silence followed as they looked at each other. I got the impression that a conversation was taking place silently between them, but couldn't be sure what was being said about me exactly.

Finally, my mom wiped away tears that I couldn't see, and Dad turned back to me. When I looked at him, I saw a stranger. Gone was the man who'd carried me into the ER after Duckie had accidentally pushed me out of the big oak tree in our backyard when I was eight. Gone was the man who'd taught me how to operate power tools when I was twelve. Gone was the man whom I'd loved more than any guy on the planet. He wasn't my dad now—I mean, he was . . . but he was also my warden. I'd never felt more detached from him.

"You get one more chance. Step out of line again, and we'll have to rethink how much time you spend with Ronald." Dad's jaw twitched slightly. "Got it?"

"Yeah . . . I got it."

Once the interrogation was completed, I went upstairs and hung the new cranes up beside the one that Joy had given me. Then I sat at my desk and began folding more, trying not to think about my parents and their seriously asshole threat to keep Duckie and me apart. I thought about the shrink I was supposed to start seeing soon as part of my outpatient treatment, Dr. Daniels, and how he could eat shit if he thought I was sharing any of my feelings with him. I also thought about Duckie and the fact that he knew that my dark thoughts hadn't been magically cured by some pills. He knew me better than anyone. Better than myself even.

It really irritated me sometimes.

I didn't notice how long I'd been sitting at my desk, folding paper cranes. Not until I heard my mom shout up to me, "Dinner's ready, Brooke! Come eat."

I stood on my bed and hung the new cranes. As I stepped down, I brushed them with my fingertips, sending them to flight. Then I went to the kitchen, my stomach rumbling.

Dad was nowhere to be found—probably tinkering in the garage or off doing whatever it was that dads did when they were avoiding their families. Mom had set a bucket of chicken on the counter beside smaller containers of mashed potatoes, gravy, sweet corn, and biscuits. A chef my mother was not, but she could order up fast food like a pro. It occurred to me that I hadn't heard her leave or return. Either I'd been super distracted by folding cranes or deeply lost in the hurt and anger over the idea that my parents would threaten to keep my best friend and me apart.

As I filled a paper plate, she asked the inevitable question, "How was school today, anyway? I mean, the brief time you spent there."

Nice burn, Mom. I shrugged in response. "It was . . . school."

The air was heavy with the absence of Dad and neither of us bringing it up. "Any word on what the play is going to be this year?"

I already knew where this conversation was headed, and I wasn't looking forward to the destination. She'd been trying to get me onstage since I'd first mentioned an interest in the theater back in the eighth grade, even though I'd made it clear I would rather have a supporting role backstage. It was like nothing I did was good enough for my mother. She couldn't just be proud of my decisions, she had to tweak them and make them hers. It was annoying. "I don't know. I didn't ask. Last I heard they were still debating between something Shakespeare or a musical. I think it's between *Romeo and Juliet* and *Fiddler on the Roof*. One of those, I guess."

"Have you thought about trying out for a part? Being on stage instead of heading up makeup crew? It's your senior year. Graduation is merely months away. Might as well go out with a bang."

"I don't know." I did know, just like I knew every time we had this conversation. But I also knew she wouldn't listen.

"You've been involved in the plays since the eighth grade. It would be a shame not to spend at least one play on the stage rather than behind it."

I flopped a pile of mashed potatoes onto my plate. They'd been so overwhipped, they almost looked like whipped cream. With my fork, I molded the pile into a tiny volcano before topping it off with gravy lava. The poor little sweet-corn people had no idea what was coming for them. "It's called being backstage, Mom. And I just don't feel like it, okay?"

"I think it would be good for you to get back into a routine. To keep your mind off things. That's all." She put an odd emphasis on *things*. Because in my family, we didn't utter phrases like *suicidal ideation* or *wanting to off yourself*. We smiled for the camera and pushed our pain down deep. It was just the Danverses' way.

"I said no. And before you ask, I'm not going to prom either." She looked at me as if I'd slapped her. I shook my head. "Just leave me alone."

I scooped up a few of the gravy-covered corn people and put them in my mouth. *So long, little corn people. Rest in peas.*

After a long silence, Mom cleared her throat. I was really hoping she wasn't going to push the play issue some more. I was over it. "Don't forget your therapy appointment tomorrow with Dr. Daniels. You want me to drive you?"

That was my mother for you. If I said something to upset her, she'd make sure to remind me of my flaws. What she was really saying was, *Fine, then. Don't be onstage, like I want you to. But don't forget to see your therapist, you little freak.*

"I'll get a ride with Duckie."

"You sure? Because I can take the afternoon off. Then maybe afterward we can—"

When I dropped my fork onto my plate, it landed in the potato volcano, crushing it. There were no corn survivors. I didn't even look at my mother as I stood up and started walking away. I went upstairs, closed my door, and shut out whatever fantasy she was building up in her head about whatever stupid mother-daughter bonding activity she thought would make my depression dissolve into thin air. As if taking a few pills and getting a mani/pedi would be enough to make me want to go on living. As if that was all it took to escape from the darkest recesses of my mind.

Her voice followed me upstairs, drifting through my bedroom door. "Brooke, where are you going? I was just trying to talk to you."

I spent the next several hours lying on my bed, wondering if Grandma still existed somewhere or if everything that had made her Grandma had dissipated into nothingness the moment her brain activity ceased. I wondered if after you died, you went somewhere with mansions and angels, if you just hung out and stalked the living without them realizing, or if you just . . . weren't . . . anymore. I wasn't sure what to believe, and it didn't really matter anyway. All that mattered was that I would be free of this pain, free of this existence, and on to something else.

Once the silence of night took over the Danvers household, I slipped quietly from my room and began looking for something—anything, really—to use to kill myself.

I looked all over the house—even the garage—but nothing stood out to me as a tool to end the hurt. Finally, I slumped on the floor of my bedroom, resigned to the fact that I might just be stuck in this place of nothingness and pain for a long time.

That's when I saw it.

It was as if I'd made a wish and someone or something had granted it. My parents had been very meticulous about removing potentially dangerous things from my room. But they'd forgotten one thing.

Peeking out, just barely, from behind my desk was the power cord that was plugged into the wall and attached to my MacBook Air. I crawled over to it and pulled my desk away from the wall a few inches. After unplugging it, I detached the smaller cord from the larger extension. With a deep breath, I gripped the thicker cord and gave it a good yank with both hands. It seemed pretty solid. Plus, it was just over five feet in length, so I was certain I could get a good knot around the closet bar, with plenty of room for my neck.

This was it. I was ready. Mom was sleeping down the hall. Dad was snoring in front of the television. I was alone. And I was mere minutes away from freedom.

A strange panic filled me. If I didn't do it now, they might discover the cord and remove it. If I didn't do it now, I would wake up tomorrow . . . and I just knew that my first thought would be one of regret.

I opened my closet doors and looped the cord around the bar, pulling it snug. Without thinking, without feeling, I tied the other end around my neck and stepped up on my hamper, thankful for such a tall closet. It was almost over—all my pain, all my anguish, all my absolute sorrow. I was one small step away from the freedom that I so longed for.

There was a moment, a brief one, when I wondered if it would hurt. I pictured the videos I'd watched on deeply buried sites online of people strangling themselves to death. They'd kicked and flailed, and I wasn't certain if that was just the body's natural reaction to strangulation . . . or if it was a sign of having second thoughts. I wanted to die, but I didn't want to hurt. Not a lot, anyway.

As if in a response from the universe, my left foot slipped and I fell in a short drop, dangling in my closet. The pain was unbearable. I was choking, flailing, my tongue protruding from my mouth. Images from the videos I'd seen flashed through my mind, but still, I didn't have my answer. Part of me knew that the pain would soon end. Part of me was struggling to be free of the cord, for what reason, I had no idea. Then there was a loud crash, and I slammed onto the floor. I coughed and coughed until air at last entered my lungs in a fiery gasp.

A pile of clothing and hangers covered me. The closet bar had broken. I coughed again, my lungs burning, my neck and spine aching terribly.

My bedroom door was flung open and my dad burst in, his eyes wide. "Are you okay? What happened?"

I waved my hand at him in a dismissive way, hoping I'd

be able to talk. It still felt like the cord was squeezing my throat, even though it had apparently slipped free and was nowhere to be seen. When I spoke, my voice was hoarse, my throat on fire. "I'm fine. Just tried to reach something on the top shelf and put my foot on the bar."

"Jesus, Brooke." He looked at me in utter relief that I was all right. If only he knew. And the lines in his forehead suggested that he wasn't quite certain if he totally bought my line of bullshit. His eyes scanned the closet, me, my room, but apparently his examination was enough to convince him I'd been telling the truth. "You know we have a step stool, right?"

I nodded. "I'll remember that for next time."

He wet his lips and sighed. For a moment, I thought he might say that he knew damn well what I'd been trying to do and then tell me he was taking me back to Kingsdale immediately. But instead, he said, "It's late. I'll fix your closet tomorrow. You should get to bed."

After he left, I sat in my closet and cried from the very depths of my soul. I was alone in this, and no one could save me.

Not even me.

CHAPTER FIVE

I was exhausted when Duckie picked me up for school the next morning, and my throat still hurt like hell. I also had the worst headache of my entire life. It was going to be a long day, I could feel it. Made longer by my mom watching out the front window, as if to be certain I was going with Duckie, the way I was supposed to.

I slid into the Beast and shut the door, fighting a yawn and losing. Duckie didn't put the Beast in reverse or anything. He just sat there, so I looked at him, already knowing what was on his mind. He said, "Are you mad?"

"No. I'm not mad." Duckie was pretty intuitive. I *was*

mad, but not for the reasons he might have thought. I was mad because I opened my eyes this morning. I was mad because I woke up in my bed, in my room, in my life. I was mad because I woke up at all. I wasn't mad at Duckie, or anybody else—even my parents, really. I was mostly mad at myself and feeling lost and confused.

"You don't have to talk about what happened that night at the river, y'know. Or even what happened in the hospital. I was just curious. I didn't mean to—"

"Let's just drop it." I pulled my sunglasses out of my backpack and slid them over my eyes, dimming the morning light.

Duckie didn't miss a beat. Unlike my mother, he knew when to stop. Generally. "Consider it dropped. Oh, by the way, I'll be a little late to economics today. Drama committee meeting during first hour."

"Can you give me a ride to my shrink after school?"

"Of course." He leaned closer and squinted, examining my face with his eyes. "You feeling okay? You look like you aren't feeling well. Are you sick or something?"

My throat was still burning, and the bruises around my neck hurt. Thank the fashion industry for decorative scarves. "Can we just go now?"

His jaw twitched slightly at my biting tone, and he turned the key in the ignition. "Ma'am, yes, ma'am."

He was annoyed. Or hurt. Or some other thing that I didn't feel like exploring at the moment. I rested my forehead against the window and dozed until Duckie pulled into his usual spot at the back of the school parking lot. No quick getaways today. Maybe because he was mad at me.

Still, he held the door for me once we reached the school. We headed to our lockers, the silence between us heavy. I fully expected to see "RIP" on my locker door, but the janitor had painted over it, just like Duckie had said he would. Sticking out of my locker vents was a small black envelope. I took it in my hand and shoved it inside my backpack before Duckie could see it. It was probably some new joke about me dying, which was going to get really old really fast. Duckie grabbed his books and shut his locker. He turned to walk away, but before he got four steps, he turned back again and mouthed "I-L-Y" to me.

I mouthed back to him, "I-L-Y too." Because I did.

Grabbing a seat at the back of the class next to Duckie's empty desk, I tried to will time to move forward as quickly as possible. Not that I had anywhere to be.

I pulled the black envelope from my backpack and opened it, mentally preparing myself for whatever idiocy it contained. Inside was a black piece of paper. Written on it in messy silver swirls was simply, "Thanks for the apple. — Derek."

Furrowing my brow, I read the note over again. Derek. The new guy. The one with the amazing eyes. How thoughtful of him. Or was it some kind of joke? Why the black stationery? I flipped the note over, searching for more words, but found nothing. So I sank down in my seat, fretting about why he'd left me a note over something as silly as an apple and not hearing a word that Ms. Naples had to say about economics. Duckie joined me after a few minutes, looking just as bored as I felt. I hid Derek's note in my backpack, but I wasn't sure why, exactly.

It felt like the entire world was staring at me during the next two classes. But I wasn't sure if people were actually staring or if I just thought they were staring. By the time I got to lunch, my hands were shaking. I didn't want to go home, but I didn't want to be here. I didn't want to be anywhere, really.

When I got to the lunchroom, Duckie was waiting for me with an expectant look on his face. He wanted an apology, and he totally deserved one. The moment I reached him, I gave him a hug. "I'm sorry. I had a really bad night and I totally took it out on you."

He hugged me back and when we parted, he wore a satisfied smile. "Just try to remember that I'm on your side, okay? I'm always on your side."

"I will." He walked me over to our usual spot before

he went to grab our food. I tried to be as casual as possible about searching the crowd for Derek, but I didn't see him anywhere. Duckie returned with two trays and set them on the table triumphantly. "It's nacho day!"

In case it wasn't obvious . . . Duckie really liked nachos.

Relieved that the tension between us had evaporated, I set Derek's note in front of Duckie and said, "That new guy, Derek, left this on my locker."

After reading it, he said, "That was nice."

"Yeah, I guess. But what's it mean?"

Through a mouthful of chips and cheese, he said, "Why does it have to mean anything? Maybe he was just being nice."

"Why?" I looked at Duckie, and he sat there for a moment, looking at me. I couldn't tell what he was thinking, which was rare.

"Let's ask him." Duckie picked up the note and stood, then started walking toward Derek's table.

I reached out with my right hand but missed grabbing his arm by seconds. "Duckie, don't!"

Before I could say anything else, my best friend was standing in front of the new guy, smiling. "Hey."

Derek looked a little more than surprised, which was a perfectly natural reaction to your first encounter with the Duckman. "Hey."

"So Derek. Brooke and I were just discussing the nice thank-you note you left her." Duckie tilted his head slightly just as I walked up behind him. I was hoping to drag him away before he did something stupid, but then he said, "What's it mean?"

Too late, I guess.

Derek looked confused. "It means . . . thank you."

"I'm sorry. He's being stupid." When Derek turned his blue eyes to me, my mouth went a little dry. It took me a moment to recover. "I heard you moved here a few weeks ago. From where?"

He shrugged. "A dumpy little town near Chicago. Are you new too? I hadn't seen you around until yesterday."

I shook my head. Out of the corner of my eye, I saw a strand of my pink hair and wondered what he thought of it. The weird, skinny kid wearing leopard-patterned shoes and the pink-haired freak had just strolled into his world. Did he want us there? Did it matter if he didn't? "No, I've been in this school system since kindergarten. I was just out for six weeks . . . for medical reasons."

"Been there. Got the T-shirt." A strange, almost knowing look crossed his face, and I wondered what it meant. Derek apparently inspired all sorts of questions in me.

Duckie had fallen silent, so I looked over at him. He was staring across the lunchroom at Tucker. I nudged him curiously. "What are you doing?"

"I'm willing him to talk to me. With my magical brain powers."

Tucker was seriously cute, but it was almost a surprise that he was the object of my best friend's affection. Tucker was everything that Duckie was not. He was straight As and student council. He was football team and track. Yeah, he might have been theater, but he was also yearbook committee.

I leaned closer and whispered, "Should I go ask him why he hasn't talked to you yet?"

As the words left my mouth, he met my eyes with a silent *Damn you* because he knew full well that turnabout was fair play. He sighed, dramatically, which was the only way that Duckie ever sighed. "Okay, I'm going. But you are one sadistic person, you know that?"

As he walked toward Tucker, I said, "I-L-Y too, Duckie."

Derek said, "You two a couple?"

I had to fight to suppress a laugh. "No."

He nodded as if he understood. I hoped he did. There was nothing that I hated more than outing my best friend to people who didn't know him. "His name is Duckie?"

"It's his nickname. Kind of a long story, but we're both pretty obsessed with this movie from the eighties called *Pretty in Pink*. His real name is Ronald, but no one but my parents and the old hag in the office really calls him that. Not even the teachers."

Derek raised an eyebrow. It was okay. I knew we were weird. No need to remind me. "Is that why you dye your hair pink? Because of the movie?"

This was the part where he'd either decide that Duckie and I were interesting enough to continue speaking to in the future, or strange enough to be avoided from here on out. "No. I just did that to piss off my mom."

He smiled at that. "What class do you have next?"

"Gym. You?"

"Chemistry."

A weird silence fell between us. I swallowed hard, guessing our conversation was over. "Well, I'll see you around."

"Yeah. See ya."

I spent the remainder of the school day thinking about that stupid thank-you note and wondering what it meant. There was no way it could have just meant "thank you." Who sent thank-you cards anymore? It was bizarre.

After school, Duckie drove me twenty minutes to Dr. Daniels's office. He pulled the Beast into a spot and put it in park before asking, "So should I go in with you or—"

"No." The word had snapped out of my mouth like the crack of a whip. I immediately felt terrible for how it seemed to make Duckie feel. But he couldn't go in with me. I didn't want him to view me as someone's crazy patient. It was bad enough that Dr. Daniels had stopped in my room at Kingsdale to introduce himself the day after Joy had offed herself. I didn't talk much during that little visit. But he did. He told me that Joy had been a high-risk patient of his for a long time. He told me that suicide is contagious, but that he thought that I was stronger than Joy had been.

As far as I knew, Dr. Daniels would always think of me in that white room, wearing scrubs, taking pills to numb the pain and help me rest. I couldn't have Duckie thinking about me that way. I just . . . couldn't. "Just wait here, okay? I'll be out soon."

He nodded as I exited the Beast. I knew he was hurt, but I didn't know what to do about it.

Minutes later, I was seated across from Dr. Daniels in a cozy floral chair. He handed me a bottle of water and smiled. "How are you today, Brooke?"

"I'm okay."

The look in his eyes said that he knew I was lying. I didn't really give two shits. "You started back in school again recently, right? How's that been?"

"It's been fine." *We could go back and forth all day, doc.* I really didn't care. I was only at the appointment because the psychiatric team at Kingsdale Hospital had insisted on weekly therapy for at least six months, and my parents agreed. I wasn't planning on being around that long.

Dr. Daniels shifted in his chair a bit, as if getting comfortable. He knew he was in for a tough time convincing me to open up. I could see it in his eyes. "Tell me about it."

I shrugged his question off. "What's to tell? It's school. I get up, go to class, go home."

"High school can be pretty rough, even in the kindest of circumstances."

Truth, doc. Truth.

"What was your first day like? Walk me through it."

"It was short and obnoxious. So I left early." I was trying to annoy him, but it didn't seem to be working. If he were my mother, the conversation would have ended two questions ago. But the doc was cool as a cucumber. He must do this for a living or something.

"Why? Did something happen?"

I debated not telling him about the graffiti on my locker, or the scribblings on my notebook, or the stupid funeral invitation. After all, he was just going to ask me how I felt about those things, and I'd had about enough of that stupid question. Every day, a couple times a day, while I was serving my time inpatient, someone would ask me how something made me feel. The biggest feeling I could recall having was inspired by them asking how I felt—pure, unadulterated anger. Frankly, it pissed me off that they wouldn't let it go.

Thinking about the inpatient facility brought the acrid smell of antiseptics to mind. I could almost smell it—just a wisp—and then it was gone.

He looked at me expectantly, awaiting a response to his question. When I didn't give one, he said, "Okay, then. You don't seem to feel up to talking much. So why don't we do something else?"

As calmly as ever, Dr. Daniels grabbed a game of Monopoly from a shelf in the corner and began setting up the board between us. As he passed out the money and set the cards in their respective places, two things happened: A. I seriously began to question his approach to therapy. And 2. I found myself feeling a little more like answering some of his questions. Not a lot of them. Just the facts, ma'am.

After a moment in which I debated what he was up to with this whole Monopoly thing, I scooted forward in my seat and reached into the box. I picked up the little metal thimble and placed the top hat on its dimpled end, making it look like a tiny, faceless gentleman. I don't know why. I'd always used that as my play piece, for as long as I could remember. Then I set my little dude on Go and bit the inside of my cheek. Hard. "Someone wrote something on my locker *my first day* back. And then someone else—or maybe the same person, I don't know—wrote it on my notebook later that day."

I didn't bring up the funeral invitation. It felt like too much, for some reason.

The doc chose the race car. I instantly wondered what kind of vehicle he really drove. I was guessing it was either a sedan or an SUV. The man was wearing khakis, for goodness' sake. Race car? Puh-lease.

When he spoke, his tone sounded so casual, but I could hear the hint of interest in between his words. "What did they write?"

"RIP." What was I doing? Hadn't I sworn to myself that I wasn't going to give any information to this shrink? Before I knew it, my mouth decided to keep talking. "Y'know, like on gravestones. Rest in peace."

"Wow. You go to school with some real winners, eh?" He looked at me, and I could tell that he could relate. *What did the kids in school pick on you for, doc? Why don't we talk about your issues for a while?*

I shrugged and rolled the dice. "If by *winners* you mean *assholes*, then yeah."

As I moved my piece, the doc said, "Do you think people know about your suicide attempt?"

"It feels like everybody knows." I sank into the seat cushion some, wishing I were anywhere but in this room. I didn't want to play Monopoly with some sedan-driving, khakis-wearing loser, let alone tell him my deepest, darkest feelings.

The doc rolled the dice and moved his piece forward, claiming a railroad. He looked a little triumphant as he picked up the card. *Way to go, doc. You may have lost at high school, but you win at Monopoly.* "Why do you say that?"

"Because I can see it in their eyes and hear them whisper every time I'm around." My words came out sharper than I intended. So I took a breath and tried to keep my cool. No need to let the doc see how much something bothered me. "Besides . . . small town. Y'know? Gossip travels at lightning speed."

The doc was quiet for a moment. He was looking at me as if weighing how to get inside my head. *Best of luck, doc.* "Is it possible that you're so concerned that they might find out about your attempt that you're sensing something that isn't there?"

"Isn't it also possible that therapists are full of crap and just guessing at the problems and potential solutions of strangers?" I said it to hurt him, and I hoped it did.

But to my great shock, a smirk appeared on his face. "I suppose anything is possible."

Maybe the doc knew that therapists were generally full of crap and khakis were a poor fashion choice. Maybe he knew, but didn't care. That was actually pretty cool. "I suppose it is."

I rolled the dice again and moved four spaces. My faceless thimble gentleman was just visiting the jail. But at least he wasn't locked up inside. At least he was free.

My mind turned back to the inpatient facility again. It had been a lot like how I imagined prison must be. Someone was always around. Someone was always watching. But even though people constantly surrounded you, it was so damn lonely.

The doc picked up the dice and held on to them for a moment. When he spoke, his words were hushed, as if I was a nervous woodland creature and he didn't want to startle me. "Do you ever think about attempting suicide again, Brooke?"

It was ballsy of him to ask, but I wasn't surprised that he had. That was why I was here, wasn't it? To keep answering that question until someone in the psychiatric community believed me and gave me a pass back into the real world, where no one had to tell anyone how they felt? I took a breath before I responded. The lie was so easy, so familiar to me now that it was like a second skin on my tongue. I tried to make it sound natural, but both in my head and out, my words sounded practiced. Almost robotic. "No. I just want to get better."

Dr. Daniels paused, eyeing me for a moment before speaking. He knew I was full of shit. He rolled the dice and got a six. As he moved his piece slowly from square to square, he said, "Are you certain? This is a safe space, Brooke. You can say anything to me, and it's just between us. And I assure you, there's nothing you can say to me that would shock me or surprise me. You shouldn't say you're not feeling suicidal if you don't mean it."

When Duckie and I were little, there was a poem we used to say whenever the other was lying. *Liar, liar, pants on fire, hang them on a telephone wire.* Duckie's child voice filled my head with that song as I sat there in the doc's office, wishing I were anywhere but there, wishing that people would stop asking me questions or at least not be so damn troubled by the truth that I couldn't tell them. With Duckie's singsong voice filling my head, getting louder and louder with every refrain, my even temperament broke for a moment and I knocked the game board over, sending playing pieces and cards and rainbow-colored money all over the floor. The doc looked mildly surprised, but not as shocked as I'd hoped. I scooted forward in my seat and gave him the hardest glare I could muster. "I swallow the pills they prescribed me at Kingsdale, don't I? I came here to see you and play goddamn Monopoly. I'm answering every stupid question you ask of me. What do you want, a legally binding contract swearing

I don't have those thoughts sometimes? Because I can't give you that. And expecting me to is about the dumbest thing I can imagine."

He sat forward too, mirroring my posture, but not my tone. His was calm and even. "This isn't like some list where you can check things off, Brooke. Therapy is a process. It takes time. I want to help you."

"Then move the hands on the clock forward about thirty minutes." I held his gaze, daring him to speak again, to say one more stupid shrink thing. A long silence hung between us before he finally broke it.

He looked disappointed. Not in me, but in his seeming inability to make me grasp his checklist bullshit. "You seem aggravated."

What I wanted to say was *And you seem like a nosy asshole with a framed diploma on the wall*. But what I said instead was "Check your clock, doc. I think our time is up."

I stood and hurried out of the office as fast as I could, slamming the door behind me. As I passed his reception-ist's desk, she opened her mouth to ask me about arranging my next appointment, but I cut her off with a curt "No."

When I stepped outside, I was relieved to see that Duckie was still sitting in the Beast, ankles crossed and feet on the dashboard, listing to some Concrete Blonde. He jumped when I opened the passenger-side door and got inside. Then he turned the volume down and said, "How'd it go?"

"Fine."

He paused, as if debating whether or not to challenge my lie. Then he turned the key and the Beast's engine roared to life. I stared at my feet the entire drive, not talking, just waiting to be home. And when Duckie pulled into my driveway, I got out without saying good-bye. He didn't say anything either. Maybe he knew better.

The house was quiet but for the stomping of my feet on the stairs as I made my way to my room. The only thing I could think to do was to fold some more goddamn cranes, but as I was walking into my room, my dad was walking out holding a bucket full of random dad stuff in one hand and a power drill in the other. "Fixed your closet. Clean up that mess now. And for the love of all hell, use a step stool next time, would ya?"

"Yeah, Dad. Sorry. Thanks."

It had occurred to me when I was about thirteen that my dad never really said "I love you." Not with words. He'd say it by fixing stuff that was broken and teaching me how I could do cool stuff like build small rockets that we'd set off in the backyard or blow up those little green army men by duct-taping them to firecrackers. He might not have said he loved me—not many times, at least. But stuff like him repairing my broken closet was about as good it got.

It took me over an hour to put all my clothes back on hangers and organize my closet. As I was sliding my hamper back into place, I noticed something sticking out of the thin space between the wall and the floor trim. It was shiny and metal, and when I realized what it was, my heart jumped inside my chest.

It was the razor I'd hidden there. Mom and Dad must have missed it during their sweep of the house.

I sat there for a moment, staring at its edge, thinking about the doc and what a dick he'd been.

Then I slowly closed my closet doors, leaving the razor where it was for the moment, sat down at my desk, and folded some goddamn origami cranes. Maybe I was hoping to find some quiet, some calm. But instead there was just anger and bitterness boiling up inside of me. At my parents for turning my house into another inpatient facility. At Dr. Daniels for thinking he knew so much. At Joy for succeeding where I'd failed. But mostly at myself for being naïve enough to think I could take away all my pain in a single night. With a single step. Into a single body of water.

Other people seemed to think that most suicidal people had just one reason to feel the way they did—a distinct, clear moment in time that they could point to and say, *Aha! That's when it happened. That's when I decided I wanted to die.* But it wasn't like that for me. It was like being slowly chased by this shadowy thing that refused to go away. There was no rhyme. There was no reason. There was no childhood trauma or sexual assault to blame it all on, no substance-abusing parents or relentless bullying experiences. There was just me. With my fucked-up brain. And some old man who'd decided that I didn't deserve any kind of release.

I hung the new cranes over my bed next to the old ones. They waved at one another with their tiny little paper wings, already friends.

Tears rolled down the sides of my face, soaking my hair. I watched the cranes until sleep finally came. And just as I was slipping into unconsciousness, I couldn't help but thank the cranes for understanding that though I was crying, I had no idea why—and the night for bringing me at least a small taste of the darkness that I so richly craved.

CHAPTER SIX

After school the next day, I was standing outside, waiting for Duckie, watching all the cars and buses pull out of the parking lot. Tucker had asked him to help out with moving some of the stage supplies from the auditorium to the shop class, so naturally, Duckie had said yes. I was perfectly content to wait on the sidewalk near the Beast while they spent a little time together. Duckie needed to make a move—and if he wasn't going to, I was hopeful that Tucker might.

From behind me came a familiar voice: Derek's. "I heard something about you. I'm not sure if it's true or not, and I don't believe in listening to rumors."

My heart skipped a beat, and the new cranes that I'd folded that day began whispering excitedly inside my backpack. I told them to hush. "Oh yeah? What did you hear?"

He withdrew a pack of smokes from his inside jacket pocket and popped an unlit cigarette into his mouth. As he pulled a Zippo lighter from his front jeans pocket, he said, "I heard you tried to drown yourself."

I shrank inside myself for a moment. The cranes in my backpack went silent.

He sucked in, drawing the toxic fumes deep into his lungs. For a second, he closed his eyes. The look on his face was a frozen moment of pure bliss. Strange how someone who was slowly poisoning himself could look so happy about it. But then, maybe that was the point.

Derek locked eyes with me. There was no judgment in his expression, no mockery. Merely curiosity. "True? Or not true?"

I didn't respond right away, but I did immediately wonder who'd told him. I wasn't sure I wanted to respond at all, really. I didn't owe him anything, this boy who had found his way into my life somehow. Not a damn thing. But after counting three of my heartbeats, I heard myself say, "True."

He nodded slowly, looking like he was debating the sanity of the thing I'd just admitted to. He returned his lighter to his pocket, and when he did, his right sleeve slid back a little. The leather cuff he wore on his wrist moved with it. Just long enough to expose a scar. "Why?"

I swallowed hard. Was this the reason he seemed so curious about me—why he was bold enough to ask me outright if I'd tried to kill myself? Maybe this was something we had in common. Maybe not. I nodded to his wrist, feigning confidence and a certainty that I did not feel. "Probably for the same reason you have that scar on your wrist."

"You ran through a sliding glass door too?" He tilted his head, his eyes widening some at my words. I felt like a complete idiot. Why had I assumed he'd cut his wrist on purpose? Was my brain hardwired to see the urge to die in people all around me? Not everybody was as screwed up as I was.

But after a second, the corner of his mouth lifted in a smirk. "Kidding. That's just what I tell people when they ask about my scars. It's amazing what an excellent liar someone can become just for want of being left the hell alone, isn't it?"

He removed the leather cuff, turned his right wrist over, and pulled up his sleeve so I could get a better look. The scar was fairly straight, and thicker than I'd thought it would be. It ran from where his hand met his wrist up his arm about four inches. He'd meant business, that was for certain.

Without thinking, without asking, I reached out and ran

my fingertips along the raised pink line, feeling its smooth-ness against my skin. He felt warm to the touch. "You did it the right way."

"Down the road, not across the street." I'd heard the phrase dozens of times—referring to the proper way to cut your wrists so it was less likely that the doctors could save you—so I had no idea why his casual utterance of it bothered me. "Of course, the other one's not so pretty."

He put the cuff back on his right wrist and slid his left sleeve up, exposing a second, jagged scar.

Even though nobody else was around, I kept my voice low. This wasn't a conversation for anyone but those who had been there, to that dark place. "Why didn't you finish?"

"Couldn't hold the blade steady enough to do the second one. I was losing blood fast, kept getting dizzy—which is why that scar's all fucked up." The scar on that arm looked more like a lightning bolt and wasn't as long as the other. As he pulled his sleeve back down, he said, "You a cutter?"

I knew I had no business feeling offended, but I did. As if there were something nobler about hacking away at your own flesh than drowning yourself. "No. Not . . . not nor-mally. I mean, I did it once, but . . ."

I never thought of myself as a cutter. But three pink lines marked my left arm. I hadn't been trying to reach my veins, to slash my wrists, to die in such a bloody way. It wasn't suicide then. Not yet. That was months before my actual serious attempt to die.

Derek nodded to the three lines on my left arm. "Harder than it seems, isn't it?"

"Yeah. I just . . . wanted to feel something, that's all. I guess. I don't know."

He took a drag on his smoke and had the courtesy to turn his head away from me to exhale before meeting my eyes. "But you didn't feel anything. Not enough, anyway. And so you decided to end it."

"Something like that." The tiny hairs on the back of my neck stood uncomfortably on end. "You speak pretty openly about the subject. What are you, some kind of peer counselor? Is this the part where you tell me I have a lot to live for? That you and I are survivors? That life is hard, but it gets better if you let it?"

"If I really believed life could get better, do you think I would have slashed open my veins with a pocketknife?" His words were matter-of-fact. No bullshit. Derek spoke in a way that he knew I would understand. In a way that only a person who's been consumed by the darkness of depression can possibly understand.

"Depression's a bitch, isn't it?" I said.

"Almost as much as life."

For some reason, his response made me laugh a little.

What a ridiculous conversation. I couldn't talk to Duckie, my parents, or Dr. Daniels about any of this. But here I was, sharing intimate details about my darkest thoughts with a boy I didn't even know. And I wasn't sure I wanted the conversation to end. It was nice to feel understood. "Why a pocketknife and not a razor?"

He shrugged, tapping ash from the end of his cigarette. "Availability, mostly. I had the pocketknife on me, and I wasn't in a waiting kind of mind-set. I wanted it over, and I wanted it over right then. At first, I didn't think the blade would be sharp enough, but it's amazing what you can accomplish when you're determined, isn't it? It only takes a pound of pressure to slice into human skin."

"So I've heard." Images flashed through my mind. My left wrist. The blade. How hard I'd sliced into my own flesh with barely anything to show for it. Maybe I was just weak. Physically. Emotionally. I shifted my feet, wondering how much longer Duckie would be gone. Not that I wanted him to return anytime soon. I was actually enjoying Derek's company. "So what stopped you?"

"UPS guy saw me through the window after I passed out, broke in, and called nine-one-one." He said it with such casual flair, as if attempted suicide was something that people discussed every morning over doughnuts and coffee. I was honestly grateful for his tone. Most people spoke about it while shaking their heads and looking mournful. Derek didn't seem to give a shit about pretense. "Y'know, just a tip, but it's pretty impossible to drown yourself on purpose."

What was this? First the thank-you note, and now this bizarre conversation? When I spoke again, I felt my guard going back up. "Not when you down a bottle of sleeping pills first."

"Huh. That'll do it, I guess." He paused to take a final drag on his cigarette before dropping it to the ground and crushing it with his boot. The sight of his jawline was almost mesmerizing. He didn't offer me a smoke. Maybe he sensed that I just wasn't the type of person who smoked. Maybe he didn't think about whether or not I smoked at all. As he blew out the smoke, he said, "So what went wrong?"

I sighed, suddenly wishing the subject would change. "Some old man was out walking his dog that night. He saw me jump into Black River and pulled me out."

"Fuckin' heroes, man." He shook his head. "How long were you inpatient?"

"Too damn long. Six weeks."

"And now everyone treats you differently." There was no question in his tone. Just understanding. He must have done inpatient time too. You don't cut your wrists that deeply and get sent home after a few stitches or staples.

"Yeah." I wanted to say more, to talk about how much it hurt to be treated like the town freak. But I didn't trust him yet. I didn't trust anybody anymore. Especially myself.

Out of the corner of my eye, I saw Duckie exit the front of the school. Derek followed my eyes to my approaching best friend and took a step closer to me. Maybe he felt the same way that I did about other people not understanding. "They have to treat you differently, you know. You are different. You've been to a place they can't even wrap their heads around."

I looked at his wrists. With his sleeves down, his leather cuff on, I couldn't see his scars, but I knew that they were there. Shoving my hands in the pockets of my jacket, I spoke—my voice hushed, as if we both shared a secret. Which, when I thought about it, we did. "But you've been there. You've been to that place."

"If you mean I've peered into the darkness and seen what lurks on the other side? Yeah. Yeah, I have. So I guess we have that in common." He smiled, and I wondered what his lips might feel like against mine.

As Duckie approached, just yards from us now, I said, "Thanks for the talk."

Reaching out, he took my hand in his and pulled a marker out of his back pocket. Then he wrote a phone number on my palm and said, "My cell. In case you ever feel like talking."

I took the marker from him and wordlessly wrote my number on the back of his hand.

Derek started to turn away. Still wearing that same smile on his lips, he said, "Welcome to the afterlife, Brooke Danvers."

CHAPTER SEVEN

The rest of the week flew by—probably because school was boring and my mom kept me busy weeding the flower gardens all weekend. Duckie was happy to come over and help, but even someone as funny as Duckie couldn't brighten the mood at Casa de Danvers. My dad spent much of the weekend in the garage, but I was pretty sure he wasn't really fixing or building anything. He was avoiding me. Because I wasn't his daughter anymore. I was just a painful reminder that he'd failed as a parent.

Before I knew it, it was Tuesday again, which meant another fun-filled hour of getting my head shrunk. Fidgeting in my seat a little, I glimpsed the crappy, outdated magazines on the table next to me. Nothing but Hollywood gossip rags, with not one book in sight.

I hated the smell of Dr. Daniels's waiting room. It smelled like old magazines and the dusty, fake Ficus tree that stood in the corner. But worse than that, it reeked of desperation. One by one, patients would enter the door and close it behind them, flitting a glance around the room to see if they were alone. But they were never alone. No one was ever alone. And no one ever spoke. We all just sat there in shame and hopelessness, occasionally thumbing through an old copy of *People* magazine or messing around with our phones. I didn't know why the rest of them were there, but I knew that none of us thought we were fixable and that all of us thought we were somehow better than everyone else in that room. Like, I might be crazy, but not as crazy as the lady in the corner muttering to herself, and certainly not as crazy as the old man with his eyes locked solidly on his untied left shoe. Maybe I was nuts. Maybe I was unfixable. But at least I wasn't them.

Maybe that made me a bitch.

Maybe the doc had a pill for that too.

The small glass window slid open and I heard the receptionist say, "Brooke Danvers?" And then it was time for the walk of shame.

There was something so terrible about standing up in the waiting room when your name was called and making your way to that window. Whether or not it was true, it felt like every eye in the place was on me, judging me, wondering why I was here. And why wouldn't they? I was judging them. Maybe I deserved it.

I handed over my insurance card and followed the receptionist's nod to the now-open door, where Dr. Daniels was standing. He wore a kind smile—the sort I imagined a predator wore right before it struck its prey.

Yeah, I was being dramatic, but what did you really expect from a crazy person?

To go along with his killer smile (pun intended), he wore khaki pants (again), a white shirt, a dark blue tie, and a tweed jacket. As we stepped inside his office and he closed the door, he said, "Good afternoon, Brooke. How are you?"

I sighed. "Crazy, apparently. Otherwise, why would I be here?"

He shook his head and offered me a bottle of water. "You're not crazy. You may be struggling with mental health issues, but that doesn't make you crazy."

"So what does?" I took the water from him, but I knew I wasn't going to drink it. Was he worried I'd get dehydrated from crying? *Not likely, doc. Not likely.*

"That's a good question." He took a sip of water from his own bottle and said, "Typically, when someone is referred to as 'crazy,' they're considered mentally deranged in a really aggressive manner. But I don't care for the word. It's outdated and insulting. It insinuates that whatever is going on with a person cannot be treated. I don't believe in that. I believe that with enough time, effort, behavioral modification, and possibly medication, everyone with mental health issues can be helped."

I stared at him for a moment. Then decided to call him on his bullshit. "So you're saying I can be cured. Pardon me, doc, but I think that's a load."

"I never said you could be cured. I said you can be treated."

"And the difference would be?"

He sat forward and met my eyes. I hadn't noticed during our last visit how young he seemed. He couldn't be out of his thirties yet. He said, "You have clinical depression with suicidal tendencies, Brooke. Think of it like having diabetes. You'll always have these health issues, but they can be managed. You can go on to live a happy, normal life with the proper treatment. You will never be cured, but then, there's nothing to cure. Just something to treat."

I sat there for a moment, hating that the doc was offering

me a tasty treat of possibility and really hating that I was tempted by it. He couldn't help me. No one could. "You think you have all the answers."

He smiled, seemingly charmed by me. I hated him for it, but liked him at the same time. Then I hated myself for liking him. "So, let's get on with our talk. How's everything at home?"

Good. Back to business. "Peachy. Perfect. Rainbows and sparkles."

"Brooke."

"Let's just say it's being managed."

He frowned at my snotty remark and said, "How's your dad handling things since you've been home?"

"He isn't. He spends a lot of time in the garage when he's home, and won't even look me in the eye. And my mom is watching my every move . . . when she's not giving me chores to keep me busy." I hadn't realized that I'd yet to sit down in the floral chair until that moment, when I found relief in the fact that I was standing. I raised my voice, hoping to drive my point home for him before I got the hell out of there. "Is that what you want to hear? That my home life sucks? Because it doesn't, okay? I have a typical family and a typical life."

"That sounds—"

"Don't, okay? Don't say something all shrinky or psycho-analytical or any crap like that, okay? Because I don't want to hear it." I was almost shouting. I wondered if any of the people in the waiting room could hear me.

The doc lowered his voice to a really calm tone, probably in an effort to chill me out. "I was going to say that that sounds like a pretty shitty way to treat their daughter after she's just been through one of the most painful experiences I can even imagine."

I knew where this was headed. Textbook. "You mean a suicide attempt."

"No. Surviving it." He held my gaze after he spoke, and I felt surprise fill me again.

I stood there for a moment, and then took my seat in that damn floral chair. Who had picked this thing, anyway? A guy wearing khakis, that's who.

I looked at him—not his khakis or his office or the stack of board games on the bookshelf, but the man himself—and had the urge to tell him the truth. But I had to check something first. "You can't tell anyone what I say in here?"

"Not unless I find you're in immediate danger."

"So . . . not my parents? Not my school? No one?"

"No one. You have my word." His tone was totally chill, as if he'd had this conversation before. Maybe he had.

I bit my bottom lip for a second before speaking. "If you want to know the truth, I don't like coming here, doc."

"I know you don't. But I'm glad you are." He sat back in his seat, not even a glimmer of hurt in his expression. "So. What about your friends? How are they treating you since you've been home?"

I pinched some of the floral fabric between my fingers, avoiding the doc's gaze. Being honest was hard. "I don't really have any anymore. I mean, it's not like I'm hated or anything. I know people at school. But friends? I don't have any since I got back. Except Duckie, of course."

"I see." He didn't even flinch at my best friend's nickname. "Have you and Duckie discussed your attempt in any kind of detail?"

I shook my head. "Not really. I'd rather not talk about it. To anyone. Especially him."

"I have to ask, but is he, by chance, a love interest?"

That got my attention. I looked at the doc and resisted a laugh. "No way. Duckie's as gay as it gets. We're best friends."

"So you've no love interests at all, then?"

"It's creepy when you say 'love interest,' y'know. Sounds all pervy." He wilted a bit at that, as if considering it. An image of that stupid thank-you note flashed through my mind. I bit my bottom lip for a second and then said, "There is this one guy that I just met. He's . . . interesting."

The doc raised his eyebrows briefly. "These sound like some pretty positive feelings that you're experiencing. And no matter how small those bits of positivity may be, they matter."

I rolled my eyes. "I didn't say I had positive feelings. I just said I thought a guy is interesting."

He held my gaze for a moment before I tore it away again. "You don't have to agree with me. I just want you to think about it."

Now that I sat and looked at it, the office was actually really well decorated. Even the floral chair fit in with the décor. I wondered if the doc had hired a decorator or done the deed himself. I still just hated it because I hated the idea of therapy, which extended toward everything surrounding therapy—even floral chairs. Even the doc. It wasn't his fault that I hated him. It was mine. I was broken, and didn't want to be repaired.

The doc leaned forward with a look of concern in his eyes. "I have to ask you another question, and it's probably going to be painful for you to hear it. You may not want to answer, and that's okay. But knowing your history, I have to ask again. Okay?"

Here it was—the question that I knew he'd continue to

ask me every time I came to see him. The question I didn't want to answer, but was ready to. "Ask."

"Do you want to live, Brooke?"

I raised an eyebrow at him. "Honestly?"

"Honestly. Between you and me. It doesn't leave this room." On his left hand he wore a simple gold band. I wondered what kind of person would marry a therapist. Probably a really honest, well-adjusted person.

I swallowed hard and said, "No. I don't."

The doc sat back in his chair, his voice calm and full of gratitude. "Thank you for trusting me with that."

I raised an eyebrow at him. "So . . . what? You're not going to give me some bullshit list of reasons to live? Or point out all the people's lives I'd destroy by offing myself?"

"That's not why I'm here."

"Then why are you here?"

He looked at me, and for the first time, I didn't see some nosy shrink. I saw a man who had a family or at least a spouse, who wanted to help people. He wasn't like anyone else I'd met through inpatient. The doc actually did give a shit.

He said, "I'm here to listen to whatever it is that you decide to share with me. And to appreciate the fact that you've given me a moment of your time."

Suspicion filled me. It sounded too easy. "And if I don't want to talk?"

"I play a pretty mean game of Monopoly. You know. When my opponent doesn't throw the board on the floor." We both chuckled at that.

"Hey, doc?" I wanted to let him know that it was okay, that I got that he wasn't like the rest of the therapists out there—or how I assumed they were. It was the least that I could do after judging the man so harshly so quickly. He was just trying to help, after all. "Sorry I threw a shit-fit at our last appointment."

"Worse things have happened in this office, Brooke. Trust me." He instinctively touched the band on his finger, and I wondered if he was in a happy marriage. Maybe therapists didn't have perfect lives either. "Now. Tell me about this interesting guy."

"You mean my 'love interest'?" I rolled my eyes again and managed a smile.

The doc groaned and blushed slightly. "You're right. That does sound kinda pervy. I'll stop saying it. What's he like?"

"I don't know exactly."

He nodded. "Are you still folding origami cranes?"

Something twisted inside of me. I gestured to the Monopoly box and said, "Can we just play a game now and not talk anymore? Would that be okay?"

"Absolutely." The doc smiled. "But I get to be the race car."

"Can I ask why?"

He looked at me as if to say *duh* and picked up the box. "Because I'm always the race car."

CHAPTER EIGHT

A knock at our front door the next morning startled me. Duckie never knocked. He usually just walked in and announced his presence. Sometimes with show tunes. But that was Duckie.

I popped my meds in my mouth real quick and rinsed the pills down my throat with some water from the bathroom sink. By the time I reached the bottom of the stairs, my mom was opening the door. When I saw Derek standing outside, I almost swallowed my tongue. His hair was messed up in the most perfect way possible, like he'd just rolled out of bed. He was wearing jeans and boots again, but this time his T-shirt was plain black. I almost melted into a puddle, but I managed to pull myself together.

Mom didn't look impressed. "Can I help you?"

"Yeah. I'm here to see Brooke." He looked over my mom's shoulder at me. "Hey."

For a long, drawn-out moment, I didn't speak. But I eventually remembered how to form words. Even if they weren't exactly smooth words. Even if they did make me sound like some kind of robot from one of those old black-and-white sci-fi movies. "Hi. There. Derek."

Smooth, Brooke. Real smooth.

"Mom, this . . . this is Derek." She gave me a look that said she'd pretty much figured that part out. She also looked increasingly suspicious. "We go to school together. He's new."

"Nice to meet you, Derek. Are you a senior too?"

"Yeah. The finish line's finally in sight." He shuffled his feet, looking like he'd rather be talking to anyone but one of my parents. I couldn't blame him. "Anyway, I wanted to offer Brooke a ride to school today, if that's okay."

Out of the corner of my eye, I could already see Mom puffing up protectively. She looked at me with an air of distrust. "What about Ronald?"

I shrugged. "He texted a few minutes ago. The Beast won't start. So . . . do you mind?"

It was a bold-faced lie, but I practically had a PhD in bullshit at this point.

With narrowed eyes, she peeked out at the driveway. "Where's your car, Derek?"

"We'll be taking my dad's truck, actually. It's at my house, just down the road. It's warm out and we live pretty close, so I just walked over." He glanced at me and then looked back at her, shrugging. "If it's a problem, I can just—"

"No, no. It's not a problem." Leaning closer to me, she spoke under her breath with a warning. "Straight to school, then straight home."

"Of course." I picked my backpack up from beside the coatrack and slung it over my right shoulder before stepping out the door. Mom watched us through the front window until we were out of sight.

Derek whistled, shaking his head. "Man. She sure likes me, eh?"

"She and Dad aren't big fans of anyone right now. Don't take it personally."

"I wasn't." He stared forward as we walked, but every few steps, I'd steal a glance at his profile. "Ya feel like going for a walk?"

The question "Why?" hung heavy in my mind. Why would he write me that note? Why would he tell me about his suicide attempt? Why would he come to my house and ask me to go for a walk? "To school? You are aware it's like two miles away, right? I'm not sure we'll make it in time for first period."

"Who said anything about school?" He flashed a smile and winked at me. "C'mon. Live a little."

I bit my bottom lip in contemplation. Then I pulled my phone out of my pocket and texted Duckie: Do me a solid and forge a note for the office. If my mom texts you, tell her I'm fine. I'm taking the day off. With Derek. Deets later. I-L-Y.

Duckie could mimic my mom's handwriting perfectly and sign her name better than she could. He didn't do it for me often, but I knew he would this time. And that would keep the school from calling my parents again.

Once I hit send, I smiled at Derek and returned my phone to my pocket. "Got a destination in mind?"

"Do we need one?"

My phone buzzed, but I didn't look at Duckie's text. I already knew what it said. The Duckman didn't disappoint. Especially not when mysterious, hot strangers were involved.

We made our way down the road a bit before I turned and led him toward the park. It was one of only a few places I was pretty sure we could get away with skipping class. But before we reached it, Derek slowed to a stop. He bit his bottom lip briefly, something troubled filling his expression. After a brief pause, he said, "Hey, do you mind if we stop at my place for a minute? I forgot to feed my dog before I left. And he gets pretty riled up if he doesn't get breakfast on time."

"Of course. Can I meet him?"

The color washed from his face temporarily. With obvious hesitation, he said, "Yeah. Sure. Come on."

He led me a bit farther down the road to a dirt driveway on the right. It was marked by a rusted, dented mailbox. I could barely make out the street numbers on the side.

Derek's house gave me the impression that he and his family lived a nomadic lifestyle. Still-packed boxes sat on the porch in several careless piles. A few were marked on the side with the rooms in which they belonged, but apparently they hadn't made it quite that far. It was as if his family was so used to moving that they were in no rush to unpack and get settled, only to turn around and stick everything back into boxes again.

The house looked like it hadn't been washed in ages. I couldn't be certain what color the wood siding had been, but neglect, weather, and time had turned it a dull gray. What looked like a shade of white paint was peeling from the windowsills. An old dirt bike sat propped up against a tree in the front yard. A rusty truck sat in the yard to the right of the dirt driveway. The steps leading up to the front door were lopsided with age. All around those steps were discarded cigarette butts and empty beer cans. As we moved up the steps, Derek turned his head and spoke to me over his shoulder, without meeting my eyes. I could see his cheek was flushed. "Sorry about the mess. It's a real shithole, but it's all we can afford until Dad finds better work."

"Won't your mom care that you're skipping school?"

"My mom isn't around anymore. Not since I was six." He opened the door and a Siberian husky immediately jumped up and placed his front paws on Derek's stomach. Derek gave his head a few pats and told him to get down. When the pup tried to jump up on me too, Derek used a more stern voice. "Vikas, c'mon. Be a good boy and get down. You hungry?"

I tried not to stare, but the inside of Derek's house wasn't much better than the outside. Vikas had clearly made a meal of one corner of the couch. The sink was full of dirty dishes. And everywhere I looked, I saw full ashtrays and empty beer cans. I was guessing that Derek's dad wasn't exactly the homey type. I didn't pity Derek, or judge him. People led different lives, after all. But the way that Derek refused to meet my eyes as he got food and water for Vikas and the way his shoulders hunched up in tension said that he was embarrassed.

I walked over to where Vikas was happily gorging himself and knelt down, giving his ears a good scratching.

"He's beautiful. How old is he?"

"He just turned one. You can tell by his paws he's gonna be a big boy." Derek looked from Vikas to me, finally meeting my eyes. "You like dogs?"

"I like animals, period."

"What about guitars?"

"You play?"

He glanced up at the clock on the wall. It looked like he was doing some quick math in his head. "We've got time. Wanna see my room?"

"Time for what, exactly?"

I hesitated, but only because we'd barely just met and here I was skipping school with him, and now maybe being coaxed into his bedroom. He must have noticed my hesitation, because he smiled and said, "I just want to show you my guitar. Scout's honor."

"You were in the scouts?"

"Hell no. C'mon." The corner of his mouth lifted in a smirk as he took my hand in his and led me down the narrow hallway.

Derek's room, in direct contrast to the rest of the house, was extremely tidy. There was a record player on top of a tall dresser, and beside the dresser, on the floor, sat a milk crate full of vinyl records. I smiled at the sight of them, thinking about my own record collection.

Two posters hung on the wall. One was a black-and-white image of Johnny Cash flipping the bird. The other was a movie poster for *A Clockwork Orange*. Derek's bed was made, and sitting on his small nightstand was an unopened pack of cigarettes; a Zippo lighter with the image of a skull on it; a DVD of *American Psycho* that was missing its case; and a small, framed photograph of a woman with Derek's eyes. I could only assume that she was his mother. I didn't ask. It seemed like such an intrusion to do so. But I did wonder where she was now.

Derek picked up a twelve-string acoustic guitar from the stand in the corner and slipped the strap over his head. He sat on the bed next to me and started playing. I recognized the tune immediately. It was "Mad World" by Michael Andrews. I'd heard it when I saw the movie *Donnie Darko* and had loved it instantly. Derek's voice was sweet, the song sad. He kept his eyes closed as he sang. When he finished, he stood up again and returned the guitar to its stand.

"That was beautiful. You're really talented."

"I'm okay. It's kind of my escape from all the . . . Well." He gestured around the room, and I wondered what he meant, but didn't ask. "So what about that walk? We should get outta here before my old man gets back. He's not always in the best mood when he gets home from the graveyard shift."

I stood up and followed his lead down the hall and out the

front door. We moved down the driveway and turned toward the park. Derek kept glancing behind us as if he was seriously concerned that his dad might see us. Once we reached the entrance to the park, he visibly relaxed. We sat on top of a picnic table near Black River. For some reason, it seemed smaller in the light of day, with Derek by my side.

"Sorry about rushing you outta there. My dad's not the nicest guy."

I shrugged. "That's okay."

"No, it's not." Derek swallowed hard and said, "He drinks. And when he drinks enough, he can be a real asshole, y'know? I just . . . I don't want him to be an asshole to you."

I smiled. "I'm pretty asshole proof."

"I wish I was." He looked a little lost and a lot sad. I could relate.

I nodded toward the bridge. "You see that stone bridge over there?"

He looked for a moment before speaking.

"Is that where you—"

"Yeah." I could still feel the water on my face, the free-fall sensation in my chest as my feet left the bridge. It had been dreamlike.

"That's not too high." It seemed a bit like he was criticizing my choices, but I was probably just prickly because of the subject matter. He walked toward the bridge, and I hesitated for a solid minute before following him. As I stepped onto it, my heart felt like it might explode.

He looked at me and said, "What was it like right before you jumped? Were you scared?"

My eyes welled with tears, but I blinked them away. "I was terrified. And relieved that my life was about to be over."

In complete silence, we both watched the water rushing under us for a few minutes. After a while, he turned to me and asked, "If you were scared . . . then how do you know it was the right choice?"

"I never said I was scared of dying. I was scared that I would fail. And I did. Still feel like a ghost ever since, though. Part of me died that day, anyway. Even though I lived." I looked at him, curious if he was willing to give up a piece of his past as well. "What were you thinking when the blade first cut your skin?"

He looked thoughtful for a moment before responding. "That it was a lot harder to cut myself than I thought it would be. It's not like the movies. It's not like slice, slice, and slip away from the world. When I finally broke through, at first I thought *Finally*, and then I was surprised that I didn't just fall over and die right away. But I was more surprised by the pain. I guess I thought it wouldn't hurt, for some stupid reason."

"I was afraid of that. The pain. That's why I took all those pills and decided on drowning. I thought it would be the least painful way to go. Kinda like going to sleep."

"Why did you do it, anyway?"

"Why did you?" A heavy silence filled the air between us.

"Because I knew death was the only way out for me. Out of the hurt of it all. Out of . . . just . . . everything." When he said the last word, he gestured behind him with his arm. I didn't know what it meant. His home life? His past, maybe? "What about you?"

"I don't know. I just wanted it to . . . stop. Y'know? All of it."

For a moment, our eyes met, the sunlight reflecting off the water below. He didn't look terribly bothered by the subject matter. In fact, he looked relieved to have someone to talk to about it. Someone who wouldn't judge him. I was feeling the same way. It wasn't at all like talking to Dr. Daniels. Or even like talking to Duckie. They didn't understand. They couldn't understand. But Derek did.

As if something had just occurred to him, he raised an eyebrow at me, his eyes brightening. "Are you religious at all? Do you believe in like heaven or hell or any of that stuff?"

"No. Not that it matters." I wasn't counting the time my grandmother had forced me to attend a summer Bible-study camp for a week when I was twelve.

"Yeah, me neither. What do you think's on the other side

of death? I bet it's just black, y'know. Just . . . emptiness."

"You ask a lot of questions."

"Does that bother you?" He pulled a packet of cigarettes from his hoodie pocket and popped a cig into his mouth. He lit it, then inhaled. The ember brightened. As he exhaled, I tried to ignore the acrid smell of it. Smoking was a disgusting, unhealthy habit. But it did give Derek that bad-boy appeal. I was a fan of that, at least. I just wished he could achieve it with something that wouldn't make his clothes smell and his lungs turn black.

"It's a little obnoxious. But I don't mind so much." I shrugged, trying to keep things casual, despite the fact that I could feel the unsettling, familiar creep of anxiety crawling its way up my spine to the back of my skull. "Can we talk about something else now? I just . . . I don't want to talk about my attempt anymore for the moment, okay?"

He inhaled again, watching me closely, as if I were a puzzle that he was trying desperately to solve. He exhaled another puff, the smoke rolling out into the air like an eerie fog, then said, "Why not?"

"Because I'm kinda trying to forget about it."

"Maybe that's your problem. That darkness is a part of you, just like my darkness is part of me. You can't just forget it, Brooke. None of us can."

I rolled my eyes. Like I needed someone else in my life to

analyze my every move. "Thanks, doc."

"I just know what you're going through, that's all." He inhaled again, blowing the smoke out slowly, thoughtfully. His eyes lowered to my mouth and stayed there for a while, as if he was thinking about what it might taste like. Seeing that sent a delicious thrill through me. When he spoke, it felt like he was standing so much closer to me than he had been, even though he hadn't moved an inch. "So are you going to kiss me or what?"

I straightened my shoulders, forcing my attention away from his lips. "I don't kiss guys who smoke."

Looking into my eyes, he took one last, long, slow, deep drag on his cigarette. He held the smoke in his lungs, closing his eyes momentarily, clearly relishing the moment. He exhaled. Then he dropped the butt to the ground and crushed it with the toe of his boot. He took a step closer to me—so unbearably, irresistibly close—and said, in a gruff voice, "Well, I just quit. So what are you going to do?"

His lips were full and pink and looked so soft. Despite my distaste for his smoking, something about it drew me to him. I wanted to taste the nicotine on his lips, on his tongue. I leaned in and pressed my mouth to his. His kiss was firm and commanding, a hint of absolute desire hidden behind the curtain of his touch. I slipped my tongue along his, and he bit it gently between his teeth, sending a sweet shock of need down my spine. He tasted like cigarettes, like motor-cycles, like electric guitars. He tasted like freedom and blue skies and rock 'n' roll.

Below, Black River rushed by. Above, a breeze rustled the treetops. The sound of water and wind and the glory of newness filled me and I could have gone on kissing him forever.

CHAPTER NINE

"And then what happened?" Duckie was sprawled out on my bed, hugging one of my pillows to his chest and grinning.

I was sitting on my bedroom floor, trying to ignore the judgmental whispers of the cranes hanging from my ceiling. They weren't happy that I'd told Derek about my past, or that kissing him had sent a wave of possibility over me. The cranes and I had made a pact to end my pain, to finish what I'd started that night in Black River. They didn't seem to appreciate my possible deviation from oblivion. But it was just a kiss . . . wasn't it?

Shrugging, I said, "We just spent the next few hours

hanging out at the park, talking. Mostly about music and kids at school and stuff like that. Then I texted you to come get me."

"The school didn't call your parents?"

"Nope. Thanks to your brilliant forgery, it looks like I'm in the clear."

"You owe me for that, by the way." He sighed dreamily. "Was there more kissing? Tell me there was more kissing. Or groping. Or dry humping. *Something.*"

Laughter spilled out of me at Duckie's ridiculous optimism. "I can't tell you what didn't happen."

He groaned, rolling his eyes. "Oh come *on.* At least lie to me and give me hope of some torrid love affair between you and the new bad boy in town."

The paper cranes folded their little wings and just looked at me with disapproval. I tore my gaze away from them and tried to focus on Duckie. "Seriously. That's all that happened. We didn't even hold hands."

The sky outside was darkening quickly as the spring storm the radio DJ had warned about rolled in. I was really looking forward to seeing the rain against my windows. There was something soothing about the rumble in the distance approaching, the speckles of water that turned into sheets, the flashes of brightness in seemingly endless dark.

The only thing better than a storm, in my opinion, was the anticipation of one.

"Was he a better kisser than Tommy Melltrigger?"

Tommy had been a sophomore-year mistake, but a great kisser. He'd also become the measurement of how good a kisser a person was. Derek had changed that today. "Definitely."

"Wow." Duckie looked at the window, and as the thunder began grumbling, he said, "The storm's coming."

Indeed, it was. The sky outside had already turned very dark gray. "What about you? When are you going to make a move on Tucker? It's senior year, Duckman. Which means you do something now or potentially never."

Duckie groaned and placed the pillow he'd been hugging over his face. Even though his voice was muffled, I could still hear him. "I can't do it. If he rejected me, I'd fall apart at the seams."

"If he rejects you, he's an idiot." I was speaking the truth and we both knew it, even though Duckie was far too modest to say it out loud. He was a great catch. And it was stupid how many guys he'd liked who'd either mocked him for it or weren't interested for whatever reason.

Duckie lay back on the bed, staring up at my paper cranes. Outside, the rain had started to fall. "I don't want much. Just somebody to cuddle with, watch movies with, text nonstop, hold hands, love me until the end of time. You know. Practically nothing."

It was a rare thing for Duckie to be serious about himself—though he had no trouble at all being serious about me. I didn't like seeing him with that look in his eye. The one that said that he felt way down deep that he'd die alone. Duckie deserved to be happy and loved. But he didn't seem to think so. My heart ached for him.

I climbed up on the bed beside him and watched the paper cranes for a while. Duckie blew at them, and they all moved slightly, taking flight. I turned my head toward him. "Planning on staying a virgin, then?"

Duckie's eyes were shiny. He blinked away his tears and said, "Hey. Not all of us just give it away without the promise of forever, you hussy."

Ripping the pillow from him, I rightly pummeled him with it while we both laughed. Yeah, I'd had sex before. Twice, actually. Once had been a mistake. The second time had been okay, I supposed. It was awkward mostly, and not exactly gratifying. Duckie knew all the details of both encounters, of course.

"You're such a wannabe hussy, Duckie."

"For the right boy, yeah." Maybe it scared boys away

when they learned that Duckie wanted to find that epic, big love before he got physically intimate with someone. Maybe it weirded them out. Maybe it made them mad. But it really made me respect Duckie for sticking to his morals. For having morals at all.

I lay my head against his shoulder. "If Tucker made a move, do you think he might be the right boy?"

"Every time I close my eyes, honey. Every time I close my eyes." The expression on his face went a little dreamy for a moment, and he finished off his thought with "Especially in the shower."

I shoved him away from me. "Gross."

Thunder clapped over our heads, cutting off the sound of his laughter. "What about Derek?"

I shrugged. The cranes looked down at me and raised their tiny little eyebrows to show that they were curious about my answer to this question as well. "What about him?"

"Would you sleep with him?"

"I don't know. Maybe. I'd definitely kiss him again." Rain was streaming down my window glass. Outside, the storm was in full force.

For a moment Duckie smiled an honest smile. I was willing to bet that he was thinking about Tucker. "So what's he like? I mean, when he's not gnawing your face into bliss?"

"Well . . . he's brave. Honest, bold, and it seems like he comes from a really rough home life." My mind flashed images—his eyes, his lips, the scars on his wrists. I furrowed my brow, wanting to share that last bit with my best friend. "There's something else too. He has these—"

"Dinnertime, you two!" My mom's voice lilted upstairs. Just the sound of it made me clench my jaw.

"Nothing. Never mind. I'll tell you later," I said to Duckie. I would. I promised myself that. Even though it felt like some kind of betrayal to Derek to tell someone else that he'd been to the same edge that I had. Even though I didn't owe Derek anything, and I owed Duckie more than I could ever repay.

To my utter shock, when we went downstairs and walked into the dining room, Dad was sitting at the head of the table. Apparently whatever had been keeping him in the garage was fixed or built or whatever for the moment. Mom set three boxes on the table and took her seat at the opposite end. Duckie and I sat side by side, facing the kitchen. We weren't a praying family—religion was just a word in the Danvers household, and only rarely ever spoken aloud. So rather than fold our hands together and say any kind of blessing, we dug in, filling our plates with slices of pepperoni pizza and cheesy breadsticks. Mom and Duckie chattered endlessly about how the play auditions had gone. It was the first audition I'd ever missed, and all because I was stuck in Kingsdale. I barely heard what they said, other than the fact that the school had decided to do *Romeo and Juliet*. I was busy trying to look at my dad without having him notice that I was looking at him. In direct contrast, he seemed to be doing all that he could not to look at me. Not so much as a peek.

I could have felt bitter. I could have been overwhelmed by anger. But mostly, I just felt sorry for my dad. And terrible for having been the cause of his pain.

"What about you, Brooke?" Mom's tone was carefully cheerful, as if she was worried that one wrong word might make Dad or me scramble from the room.

I poked at a breadstick with my finger, not really hungry. "What about me what?"

"Have you made a decision about makeup crew?" The smile she wore on her face was made of plastic and put there for Duckie—so he'd see that everything was just hunky-dory with the Danvers family. I knew that smile well. She dug it out for picnics with the neighbors and holiday dinners, or whenever we had extended family over to visit. It was like bringing out the good china. Only Mom didn't own any china. She just had that stupid, plastic smile that everyone could see right through.

I took a deep breath then and did my best to keep my tone casual. "Remember when I said I'd decided to skip it this year?"

Mom dropped her napkin on the table and looked at me like I'd just admitted to having tried heroin or something. "But it's your senior year."

I shrugged. "Look, I've had a lot going on, okay? Maybe I just don't feel like adding something else to my plate right now."

Dad said, "You should be making plans. Plans are healthy. Plans would give you something to look forward to so you can put all this nastiness behind you." He didn't look up from his plate, but I'd jumped a little when he spoke. I hadn't been expecting him to say anything to me for the duration of the meal.

"And what 'nastiness' would you be referring to, exactly?" I set my fork down on my plate and looked at my father. "Well, come on, Dad. You're finally talking to me. Why don't you say how you really feel?"

He retrieved the paper napkin from his lap, wiped his mouth, and set it on the table before meeting my gaze. "How I feel is that you should get back into your old routine and stop all this attention-seeking nonsense."

The room fell silent with the heaviness of my father's

words. For a moment, it seemed as if all the air had been sucked from the room, from my lungs, from the world. Was that what he really thought of me? That I'd merely been looking for attention? Did he really have no idea the pain and torment that I'd been lost in for the past year? Was he seriously that oblivious to the feelings of his own daughter?

I stood up slowly from the table, my eyes locked with my dad's. My chest was filled with disappointment and anger, but mostly sadness. Mom sat very still, like she had no idea what to do or say. Her plastic smile had slipped right off her face. Outside, the rain had ceased, but the storm inside our house was raging on in full force.

Ever so gently, and very quietly, Duckie said, "Brooke—"

"Go home, Duckie. I need to be alone." I didn't wait for a response—not from my best friend, not from my mom, and certainly not from my dad. I merely left the dining room as quickly as I was able to and hurried up the stairs to my bedroom. Once I'd closed my door, I leaned up against it with my back, tilting my chin up so I could rest my head against the wood as well.

Attention seeking. That's what my dad thought of me. That I was some spoiled brat who was just looking for an extra pat on the head. How could he think that about me? And even if he did, how could he say it to my face like that? What kind of way was that for anyone to talk to their daughter? Especially one who just got out of the psychiatric treatment clinic only a week and a half before.

Angry tears welled in my eyes and spilled down my cheeks.

Like rain.

CHAPTER TEN

The next few days glazed by in a blur of school and meds and faking smiles at Duckie. Then on Sunday night, I sat there on the floor of my room for hours, reliving every moment I'd spent inpatient, seeing Joy's dead eyes, wishing I could join her. Tears fell, only to be replaced with anger, then emptiness. The brief spark of hope that Derek had inspired in me had quickly withered. I just wanted my life to end. I just wanted it all to end.

The cranes whispered a reminder that the razor was still hidden inside my closet. It would be painful. It would be messy. But it would also be my salvation.

My dad's words from dinner that night still echoed in my mind. *Stop all this attention-seeking nonsense.*

Was that what everyone thought I was doing? Looking for attention? Had it never occurred to them that my pain was real, sharp, suffocating?

Opening my closet door, I slid my hamper aside. My chest was tight, and it took me a moment to realize that I'd been holding my breath. There it was, sticking slightly out from behind the baseboard. That tiny glint of silver against the white paint of the wall. I stretched out my hand, but just as my fingertips brushed the metal something hit my window.

I sat back with a jerk, wondering if it had been a bird. After a few seconds, something hit it again. I couldn't see it, but I could damn well hear it. Not hard enough to damage the glass, just enough to make a sound. I moved to the window and looked outside. Another storm had dwindled hours before, leaving puddles in the yard. Someone was standing in them, head tilted up toward my window. It was hard to make out exactly who it was due to the raindrops all over the glass, so I opened my screenless window and stuck my head out. Instantly, I recognized my middle-of-the-night visitor and was relieved that the distance and darkness would help to make me not look a total wreck. "Derek?"

His hair was wet, which made it all the more inviting.

"I'm so glad I got the right window. I had no idea what I'd say if one of your parents answered."

What a strange boy. And here he was, appearing just as I'd been about to give in and slice away my pain. "What are you doing here?"

He was wearing dark blue jeans, red Converse tennis shoes, and a black hoodie that was only halfway zipped up. It didn't look like he was wearing a shirt under it. It made me wonder if he'd just jumped out of the shower and hastily thrown on some clothes before making his way here. "I know I missed a couple of days of school, and I didn't text, but I was going to tonight. Then I thought *Fuck it* and came over. Because I wanted to see you."

My heart fluttered. He wanted to see me—even though I was a broken mess. I glanced at my alarm clock. "It's after midnight."

"So? You're awake. I'm awake. You coming down here or not?" Even from this distance, I could see the daring gleam in his eyes.

It brought a smile to my lips. "Depends."

"On?"

"Are you still smoking?"

He held up a small rectangle of silver, a smile stretching across his lips. "Chewing gum."

Without another word, I ducked back inside my room

and slipped on my jean jacket—the one covered in buttons that Duckie and I found amusing—and my shoes. I cleaned up my face in the mirror and took a deep breath. This was crazy. What was I thinking? I didn't even know this guy—not really. And if my parents caught me sneaking out, they'd lose their shit.

I climbed out the window and closed it most of the way behind me, leaving it cracked just a few inches so that I could return the same way. The roof shingles made a soft scraping noise beneath my feet as I moved down the low-pitched roof to the garage roof. When I reached the lowest point, I sat on my butt and carefully dropped to the ground, almost landing on my mom's favorite spirea bush.

Derek nodded at my smooth navigation, impressed. "I didn't realize you were an acrobat."

"Please. I've been climbing in and out that way since I was eleven. It's easier than it looks." I led him down the road away from the house, so we'd be at a safe distance from my parents' earshot. The windows were all dark, so I was pretty sure they were in bed and fast asleep by now.

When we both knew no one was around to listen, Derek said, "What adventures were you going on at eleven, exactly?"

"Mostly sneaking out to hang out with Duckie, just for the sake of sneaking out." The night air was cooler than I'd thought it would be. I buttoned up my jacket halfway and said, "Though one or two times, we went on a midnight picnic in the graveyard."

"You two seem close."

"The closest. He's my best friend." Guilt filled me for leaving him downstairs alone with my parents the other night after I'd stormed out. We had yet to talk about it, he and I. It was like he was fully aware we were standing on a frozen pond and one wrong move would ruin everything. I made a mental note to apologize the next day. "What about you? Anybody you miss from the town you left to move here?"

"Not really." He kicked a rock, and we both paused to watch it skip its way down the pavement before veering off into the gravel on the side of the road. "We move a lot, so I don't usually bother making connections. I mean, why bother getting close to people if the relationships will just end up as the equivalent of an emotional handshake, y'know? I usually stay pretty quiet and wait for us to move again."

My bullshit alarm was going off, big-time. "But you talk to me."

"You're worth talking to." He shrugged and put his hands in his hoodie's pockets. Apparently I wasn't the only one who was chilly. At least I was wearing a shirt under my jacket.

We walked along in silence for a few minutes before I

asked, "Where are we going?"

"Is it important to have a destination?"

A car approached, and we moved over to the gravel on the side of the road. Its high beams almost blinded me. I squinted against the light and waited until it had passed before I responded. "Not really, I suppose. It's just that the town of Eleos is pretty small. Easy to get caught if you're two high schoolers wandering around in the middle of the night."

"We could go back to the park." He pulled the zipper on his hoodie up a little more. But not before I glimpsed his smooth, tan chest. "Unless you'd rather avoid it."

"Why would I want to avoid it?"

"Because when we were there earlier, you looked at the bridge more than you looked at me." I stopped moving, and he came to a rest beside me. Honestly, I hadn't noticed that I'd been looking at the bridge any more than I'd been looking at him. He zipped his hoodie the rest of the way up, but before he did, I noticed tiny goose bumps over his bare chest. "Does it bother you? To see the bridge?"

"No." *Yes. Maybe.* I wasn't sure. I might not ever be. It wasn't as if the bridge had chosen my place of attempted death. I'd chosen it. Couldn't exactly blame the bridge. "It's just that . . . well . . ."

He looked into my eyes and lowered his voice a notch.

"You still think about jumping."

The little hairs on the back of my neck stood on end. I folded my arms in front of me and looked down at my shoes. With a shrug, I replied, "Sometimes. If you must know."

"It's okay. I won't tell anyone." He started walking again, slowly, and I moved in concert with him. "Besides, I get it. Sometimes, like when I'm alone at night, I have to force myself not to pick up a knife. It's not easy. And no one understands."

My mind flipped to the razor hidden in my closet. The razor I'd almost used on myself tonight. "I do."

Reaching out, he took my hand in his. Our fingers folded together naturally. It was almost as if we'd always held hands. Like our hands were made for each other.

He was looking forward, down the road, not at anything in particular that I could tell. And then, after swallowing hard, he said, "I like you, Brooke."

A small smile found my lips. "I know."

Derek threw his head back in laughter. "Oh man. I pour my heart out and she totally Han Solos me."

"Pssht. That was pouring your heart out? Hardly." My chest felt lighter than it had earlier. All of me did, really.

Derek stopped walking again and gave my hand a squeeze. His eyes reflected the moon. "The truth is, I was sitting at my house tonight, watching TV, and I couldn't stop thinking about you. The truth is, you're the first person I've ever really wanted to get to know. I know it may not seem like much, but liking you is a pretty big deal for me."

It felt like the air had been sucked from my lungs. Like when I'd jumped off the playground swings in the third grade and landed on my back, knocking the wind out of me. Only in an intensely good way. "I don't know what to say."

He took my other hand in his and leaned closer with softly spoken words. "Say how you feel about spearmint gum."

The clouds that had covered the sky earlier were gone, revealing stars. Somewhere in the distance, frogs were singing. "I love spearmint gum."

Our lips met in a kiss, and I was suddenly glad that the paper cranes were nowhere around to see it. Just for a moment, I wanted to revel in the tenderness of Derek's touch and not think about Black River or any of the aftermath. For just a moment, I wanted to feel free.

CHAPTER ELEVEN

"It's so not fair." Duckie picked a french fry from his lunch tray and stabbed it into a small heap of ketchup. He was pouting, but I couldn't blame him for it. How many times had he imagined Tucker appearing at his window one night and whisking him away in the darkness? How many dream kisses had he shared with the guy he liked? Countless, I imagined.

I took a bite of my burger and set it back down on the tray. After I swallowed, I said, "What about this isn't fair, exactly?"

"You're sneaking out at night with Mr. Perfect while I'm

staying at home watching reruns of *The Golden Girls. That's* what isn't fair."

The noise of the lunchroom was really getting on my nerves. Why couldn't people just sit quietly and eat in peace once in a while? "It's not like I planned it. And not for nothing, but you being there would have totally killed the mood."

"That's not what I mean. I just . . ." He groaned and stuffed the fry into his mouth. As he chewed, he nodded to himself and said, "I have to ask Tucker to prom."

Finally. It was about time. I'd only been nagging him since forever. "He'll say yes."

Serious, Duckie looked at me, his words hushed. "What if he doesn't?"

Reaching across the table, I gestured for him to come closer. When he did, I straightened his bow tie and said, "Then he doesn't deserve a second thought from you."

At the table next to us were a gaggle (or is it a giggle?) of fashion-focused girls and their boyfriends. One of the guys was loudly telling one of the most disgusting jokes I'd ever heard. I didn't recognize any of them. Must've been freshmen.

Duckie picked up another fry, looking thoughtful. "Is it stupid that I'm scared of him?"

I smiled and took a sip of my soda. "Not at all. It's actually kinda sweet."

The Giggle and its cohorts were all roaring with laughter. My head began to throb.

Duckie wiped his fingers and mouth clean. "Did you see they posted the parts for *Romeo and Juliet*?"

I glanced around the lunchroom for about the zillionth time, wondering where Derek was today. I was hoping to see him again and get a read on whether or not he'd meant what he'd said last night about liking me. It was hard to imagine why someone would like me. I was broken.

"No. What did you get?"

Duckie grinned. "Only Mercutio."

"Duckie! That's amazing!" The likely underclassmen occupants of the table next to ours glared at my outburst, as if I was interrupting their nice, quiet lunch instead of the other way around.

"Guess who's playing Romeo?"

He'd hoped to be the lead role our senior year, but it wasn't working out that way. "It doesn't matter who got Romeo. You're going to be an excellent Mercutio. The part suits you perfectly."

"Oh, it matters, Brooke. It matters big-time." He held up his chocolate milk carton in a toasting gesture. "Tucker is Romeo."

"Whoa. Best friends with homoerotic undertones. Nice."
I laughed, and he blushed. I hadn't seen Duckie blush in a
very long time.

"Yeah. That's what I was thinking." He turned his head,
finding Tucker in the crowd.

Placing my hand over his, I squeezed until he looked me
in the eye. "Ask him to prom, Duckie. Seriously. Do it. It's
senior year. When else are you going to have this opportunity?"

He pressed his lips tightly together and then glanced at
Tucker, who was sitting on the other side of the cafeteria. As
if sensing he was being looked at, Tucker turned his head
toward Duckie and smiled. I wasn't sure if Duckie saw it or
not. He was a bit preoccupied with fidgeting. "I was thinking about asking him tonight. They're handing out scripts
and schedules, as well as running through expectations
from everyone at seven. Are you coming?"

"Do I have to?" Of course I didn't. Duckie knew I wanted
to skip the play this year. He'd never ask me to—

"Yes."

It was like a needle was ripped off a record in my mind.
"Why?"

Duckie leaned closer and, in a loud whisper, said,
"Because you still owe me for not telling Scott Kreiger you
had a crush on him in the third grade."

My jaw dropped. "Seriously? Scott Kreiger moved away in the sixth grade. You're calling that favor in *now*?"

"You said you'd owe me a favor. And I totally could've said something. I mean, he asked me if you liked him. But I kept my mouth shut." He raised one eyebrow. It was so obvious that he was holding back his laughter at the ridiculousness of this conversation. "So, are you coming? Or are you a big, fat liar?"

Sighing with an air of reluctance, I said, "Apparently I wouldn't miss it for the world, Duckman. But this doesn't mean I'm working on the play. Oh, and if Tucker breaks your heart, I'm gonna hurt him."

"Same goes for Derek." He glanced behind me. "Speaking of which, here comes Mr. Wonderful."

Finally. I couldn't help but smile. "I thought he was Mr. Perfect?"

Duckie gasped in an overdramatic fashion. "Can't he be both?"

Derek approached the table, lunch tray in hand. He was wearing jeans and a V-neck sweater today. The sweater was dark gray and looked soft to the touch. The sleeves were pushed up to his elbows, and a white T-shirt peeked out from the V of the sweater. Something in his expression told me he was navigating unusual waters. It was like he thought we'd reject him or something. "Hey. Is it okay if I sit with you two?"

I pulled the chair out next to me. "Totally."

As Derek took his seat, I watched Duckie stare dreamily at Tucker, who had left his table to throw something away. I shouted to him, "Hey, Tucker! Come sit with us."

Tucker looked over, obviously surprised by my invitation. But he didn't shake his head or say no or anything.

Duckie turned wide-eyed to me. "You are so dead."

Under my breath, I said, "Bring it, Mercutio."

Once Tucker took a seat across from Duckie, I took the liberty of introducing him and Derek. Duckie just sat there frozen, looking absolutely terrified. Oh yeah. This was going to go really well, I could already tell.

"You heading up makeup crew again, Brooke?" Tucker stuffed a couple of fries into his mouth and chewed. In direct contrast to Duckie, who was sitting there frozen and silent, he seemed extremely relaxed and comfortable.

"I wasn't even going to attend rehearsal this year. But Duckie had a pretty convincing argument. So . . . I'm coming tonight. We'll see. No promises." That gave Duckie a small smile. Until today, he hadn't been pushing me about the play, but I knew he wanted us to be in it together. After all, it was what we did, and this was our last year of high school to do it. He knew I was going to give in and take charge of makeup. And on some level, so did I. Damn him. "By the way, I hear congrats are in order. Romeo Montague. Nothing like getting one of the lead parts senior year. Who's playing Juliet?"

Tucker beamed with pride. A slight blush colored his cheeks. "Thanks. I'm pretty excited. Teegan's playing Juliet."

Duckie deflated a little, but I was the only one who noticed. Teegan Keller had been in theater just as long as Duckie and I. She was a great actor, a fantastic singer, super pretty, smart, and one of the nicest people on the planet. Just about everyone in our school who was even remotely interested in girls wanted to date her, and with good reason.

I could already read Duckie's thoughts. What if Tucker was into girls? What if he and Teegan practiced the romance offstage and things got a bit too real? What if Duckie was about to be totally rejected by the one boy he'd ever seemed to have a real chance with?

I forced a smile, hoping Duckie would unfreeze and find his voice soon. He and Derek were both being so quiet. It was weird. "She'll be great, I'm sure. I mean, she always is, but, y'know, Juliet. It's like the part was written for her."

"Yeah, I think we'll work well together." Tucker gave Duckie's shoulder a light slap, turning his attention to him. "Hey, Duck, I saw that you're Mercutio. I've gotta say, man, he's seriously my favorite character in the entire play."

Duckie's ice façade immediately melted, and he smiled warmly at Tucker. No wonder he was into acting. He was good at it. I was the only one at the table who could tell that he was shaking on the inside. "Oh yeah? Why's that?"

Tucker shrugged. "He's funny and sassy and a total smartass. What's not to love?"

Without even realizing it—or maybe he had—Tucker had just perfectly described my best friend.

Derek hadn't said much since sitting down, so I turned my attention to him. The last thing I wanted was for him to think I didn't really want him sitting with us or that he didn't fit in. If anyone fit in anywhere, it was with theater geeks. "What about you, Derek? Ever think about working on a play? We could always use more help backstage."

We. Dammit. I was already leaning toward participation.

Derek leaned closer to me and swept a strand of pink hair behind my left ear. "Thanks, but it's not exactly my scene. If you know what I mean."

It sounded like a dig, but that couldn't be right. Though, by the looks on Tucker and Duckie's faces, they thought it had sounded like a dig as well.

The lunch bell rang and we dumped our trays before shuffling out of the cafeteria. Derek walked me to my locker with his hand around my waist. I'd never felt so safe.

Some guy was standing at my locker as we approached, black Sharpie in hand. In big, bold, black, familiar letters,

"RIP" was once more written on my locker door. Derek stepped away from me, toward the graffiti artist, and yelled, "Hey!"

The guy turned to him in surprise, and I recognized Eric Squires. Back in the day, Eric and I used to play in the sandbox during recess in the first grade. Now he was reminding me that I'd tried to commit suicide. What a tool.

Derek grabbed him by the collar and slammed him against the row of lockers. The Sharpie fell to the floor and rolled several feet away. My feet were frozen in place. Derek hissed into Eric's face, "You think that's funny, asswipe? Reminding somebody of a goddamn tragic moment in their life? You are one sick fu—"

"Back off!" Miller appeared out of nowhere, dragging Derek off Eric by his collar. "That's enough!"

Eric stood as still as stone with his back against the lockers. His face was pale and his hands were shaking. As Miller pulled Derek away, Derek met my gaze. His eyes looked dark as sin, his skin flushed in heated fury. Maybe I should have felt protected, but mostly I was frightened. Of the situation. Of the violent reaction. Of Derek.

Last night, he'd been gentle and sweet. Last night, he'd kissed me and made me feel safe. What had happened between then and now?

I didn't see Derek for the rest of the day—most likely because any kind of violence got you a one-way ticket to suspension. As usual, Duckie gave me a ride home after school. We pulled into the driveway and Duckie asked me for the hundredth time since Derek's outburst, "Are you okay?"

Of course I was. What girl wouldn't be okay, knowing her (crush? Boyfriend? What exactly was Derek to me? Did he need a label? Did he want one? What if the very word *boyfriend* scared him away?) friend was willing to risk suspension in defense of her? I was totally cool. Just peachy. Not freaked out at all. "I'm fine. Really."

He didn't look like he believed me, which could probably be attributed to the fact that I was lying my ass off. "I could always reschedule my dentist appointment if you need to talk."

"Don't be silly. I'm *fine*." I grabbed my bag and exited the car. Maybe I was fine. Totally fine. It's not like Derek had done anything to me. He was just trying to protect me.

I made my way inside through a mental fog, where I was greeted by my mother's overly cheerful voice. The one that she used whenever she was trying to make things seem perfectly normal, not the uncomfortable shit show that I seemed to inspire. "Hey, sweetie. I've been baking all day. Want something?"

"No, thanks." The last thing I wanted to do was eat. I couldn't get the look of absolute fury in Derek's eyes out of my head. "By the way, I've got rehearsal tonight. Duckie's picking me up later, after his appointment."

"You decided to work on the play after all? That's terrific!" She smiled at me, but her smile wilted some with concern. Her tone changed to one not resembling a sitcom mom's. "Are you okay? You look a little tired."

"Just a long day. I think I'll go upstairs and lie down for a while." I wandered upstairs to my room and sat on my bed. Above me, the cranes were looking uneasy, but I didn't want to hear their thoughts on the matter—any matter—at the moment. I grabbed my phone and texted Derek, but there was no response. Then I lay on my bed, reliving that moment by my locker over and over again, until Mom called me down to dinner.

Tonight's fine meal consisted of burgers and fries. I would have killed for a salad. Of course, I'd have to locate a knife sharp enough to chop up veggies first, which wasn't exactly an option in the Danvers household at the moment.

"Did you tell your father where you're going tonight?" My mom's voice was chipper as ever again. I was waiting for cartoon animals to dance into the room. I wouldn't have been surprised if they had.

Dad's face was hidden behind his newspaper once again. I cleared my throat and said, "After a lot of thought, I've decided to attend the first rehearsal of the school play."

To my immense surprise, he emerged from his newspaper fortress of solitude to join the conversation. "That's good. It'll get you out of the house. Give you something fun to do."

My chest tightened with anxiety as I opened my mouth to ask a question to which I was certain I already had the answer. "Can . . . I mean, would it be okay if I stayed over at Duckie's tonight? I know it's a school night, and I know—"

"Yeah." He nodded. "That's fine. I think you've earned it. But check in with one of us once an hour, okay? Just so we can be sure you're all right."

Mom looked nervous about Dad's decision, but all she said was "And don't miss your therapy appointment tomorrow after school."

Surprise filled me. Maybe the doors to Alcatraz were opening up at last. "I won't miss it. And I'll be sure to check in."

Mom refilled Dad's coffee mug and returned the pot to the coffeemaker on the counter. When she came back to her seat at the table, she said, "Anything new going on at work?"

Dad folded the paper up and set it next to his plate. He seemed lighter somehow. "Same old, same old. I swear, there are days when I wanna take a sledgehammer to those cubicle walls, just for some space."

The image of him wigging out and smashing his office to pieces made me chuckle. "Don't forget the outer walls, Dad. You might want fresh air too."

He leaned with his elbows on the table and smiled—for the first time that I could remember in a very long time. "Do you remember the last time we had some really good fresh air together as a family?"

After the briefest of pauses, my mom and I answered at the same time. "The cabin."

For a moment, all three of us sat there smiling. The cabin was this rustic, four-room place up north where we used to go all the time when I was younger. The nearest neighbor was two miles away. It had its own small lake and a pier; I used to sit on the end of the pier at night, watching the stars and the fireflies sparkling on the surface of the water. We'd grill fish that Dad and I would catch and clean, and we'd make s'mores every night. And when they thought I wasn't looking, Mom and Dad would steal kisses while the cicadas sang all around us.

Dad said, "We should go back there this summer. Get some good time together before Brooke starts college."

I'd almost forgotten that I'd sent an application to the University of Michigan last November. Truth be told, I'd just done it because my parents had pressured me about applying. But I knew I wouldn't be attending. I'd had other plans—plans like not living anymore. It was weird how they were acting like I was definitely going to college, considering that I only applied to the one school and hadn't heard back from them yet. But then, it was also kinda weird to still be alive.

Weird . . . but good.

Mom placed a hand over one of Dad's and gave it a squeeze—something else I hadn't seen in forever. Then she looked at me, her eyes bright with something that resembled hope. Even if it was fleeting, it was nice to see. It was nice to feel. "Oh, I'm so torn about you starting college. It's such a fun time, but can be so dangerous."

"Just major in martial arts. You'll be fine."

I laughed so hard at what Dad had said that I swear I almost shot a french fry out of my nose.

"You know, your father and I met in college. He shared the suite next to mine with three other guys."

The smirk on Dad's face said it all. "Hmm. Maybe you should go to a community college. Or a convent."

"Dad, we're not even Catholic."

"Even so." He picked up a fry and pointed it at me before taking a bite. "Just don't get so mixed up in the fun that you forget your reason for being there, okay?"

"Well, it *would* be nice to see my daughter enjoy a little romance."

It was a subtle gesture, but Dad slipped his hand out from under Mom's. "She doesn't need romance. She needs to focus on her grades and graduation."

Something in the air was changing. I couldn't define what it was, exactly, but I didn't like it.

Mom said, "I'm just saying, college is about a lot more than studying and writing term papers. It would be nice if she got the full experience."

New tension filled the air. "Just because that was your experience doesn't mean it needs to be hers, Joanne."

"Hey!" They both looked at me with utter surprise when I raised my voice. Neither seemed pleased. I couldn't give a crap. "*She* is sitting right here. And *she* doesn't appreciate having *her* life planned out for *her*. And if you're going to talk about *her*, you could at least try talking to *her* like a goddamn person."

"Go to your room, Brooke." Dad said the words so calmly. Then, as I stood, he retreated back behind the comfort of his paper. News columns were far better companions than family members sometimes, it seemed. So much for the cabin.

"I was planning on it." I stormed out and up the stairs to my room. Anywhere was better than dinner with my parents.

At quarter to seven, I heard the Beast's telltale back-fire. Slipping on my sneakers and denim jacket, I stuffed a change of clothes, a few toiletries, and some jammies in my backpack and went downstairs, ready for my dad to read me the riot act. But Dad was nowhere to be found. My mom was sitting in the living room, quietly watching some documentary about the history of quilting. She didn't say a word to me as I walked out the front door and shut it behind me, which was very weird. When I sat down in the Beast, Duckie flashed me a look of concern. "Trouble in the Danvers household tonight?"

"Nothing I can't handle." It was a lie. Well, a partial lie. I was handling things precisely as my father had been. By avoiding them. "Oh, but here's a bit of happy. My dad said I could crash at your place tonight."

Dad had probably considered changing his mind after our big fight, but even if he'd wanted to, I'd made it a point to get out of there without giving him a chance.

Duckie looked just as surprised as I'd felt when Dad had agreed. "Wow. Guess that means things are getting better."

Better. Now that was a relative term.

Duckie backed out of the driveway, and as we barreled down the road, I stared out the window, wondering exactly when my life would belong to me so I could do with it as I pleased. Maybe never. Maybe that's just the way things were.

After a minute or two, Duckie said, "What's goin' on with you? You're so quiet."

I didn't know what to tell him. I mean, he was my best friend, so of course I could tell him anything. But honestly, I just wanted to put every word my parents had said tonight out of my head. "It's not important. Just parental drama."

He accepted my answer with an understanding nod, which I was grateful for. After we parked at the school, I said, "Are you going to chicken out on asking Tucker to prom?"

Duckie rolled his eyes. His body language portrayed him as cool and collected, but I knew Duckie. Inside, he was seriously freaking out and already planning what to say if and when Tucker turned him down. "I'm not chickening out. I'm just . . . waiting for the opportune moment."

We walked into the gym, which was full of our fellow theater geeks as well as a few upperclassmen who were just looking for something extracurricular to add to their college applications. Claire Simpson was there, looking so out of place that it actually gave me a smile. People like Claire never felt out of place. Maybe it would be good for her.

The accordion walls that hid the stage along the end of the room underneath the basketball hoop had been pulled back, revealing giant red velvet curtains. The sight of those curtains was comforting, in a way. They'd marked my best times at this school, and I was taken aback by how much seeing them now really struck me.

As I scanned the crowd, one face stood out. Michael Stein. We'd headed up makeup crew as a team our freshman and sophomore years, before Michael had moved to Nebraska. He'd been dating the female lead for two years. The first night of rehearsal she'd dumped him right in front of everybody. It was mortifying for him, and we'd spent the rest of the play talking about their relationship issues. Michael was a good guy. I shouted, "Michael!"

He turned his head, and the moment he saw me, he grinned and ran over. He hugged me, picking me up off the floor a few inches before setting me back down.

"What are you doing here?" I grinned and hugged him back. I'd missed our talks. We were strictly friends, but good ones by the end of that play. *Grease.* Poor guy had his heart broken by Sandra Dee.

"I just moved back this week! What play are we doing?"

"Romeo and Juliet."

Michael wrinkled his nose. "Ugh. No musical?"

"Sadly, no."

Michael looked more than a little distracted by someone or something near the stage, and when I turned my head, I saw he was looking at Claire. "So . . . into cheerleaders now?"

"I've had a crush on her since the third grade."

I nudged his shoulder. "It's our senior year, dude. Take a risk and say hi."

As Michael beelined for Claire without another word—maybe he was worried he might lose his nerve if he didn't make his move right away—Duckie turned back from one of the sound guys and said, "Holy crap, is that Michael Stein?"

"The one and only."

"Hey, Mercutio!" Duckie and I both turned to see Tucker standing across the gym, waving an arm in the air in Duckie's general direction. I could almost hear Duckie's heart rate increase. When Tucker smiled, I was certain Duckie's heart stopped completely. "Can I have you for a minute?"

"Just a minute?" I waggled my eyebrows at Duckie, who burst out laughing and shoved my shoulder with his.

He took a deep, shaking breath and said, "I guess that's my cue, eh?"

I plucked a bit of fuzz from his vest and smoothed out some of the wrinkles before patting him on the shoulders. "Go get him, Duckman."

Duckie walked over to Tucker, looking all confident and aloof even though he was a quivering pile of goo inside. As they chatted, I was trying to figure out their conversation based solely on body language, but it wasn't easy. Then at one point, they both grinned the biggest grins I think I'd ever seen. I really hoped that Duckie hadn't lost his determination and had asked Tucker to prom. Someone deserved happiness, and of the two of us, that someone was definitely Duckie.

After a few more minutes, Duckie returned to where I was now sitting, on the edge of the stage. He appeared just as casual. Just as aloof.

I waited for a beat, but he didn't speak, so I smacked him lightly on the bicep. "So?"

"Hmm? So what?" He looked at me in a way that would have convinced anybody who wasn't me that he had no idea what I was talking about.

If he wasn't my best friend in the whole entire world, I might have strangled him right then and there. But somehow, I managed to resist. "So did you ask him or what, you brat?"

He nodded, his eyes glancing about the room before finally lowering to focus on his zebra-striped shoes. "Yep. And I have bad news."

My heart hurt. It hadn't been easy to watch my best friend go through years of heartbreak and loneliness and not be able to do anything to help him. Tucker had been the major object of Duckie's affection for so long now. I'd been certain he'd say yes. Being proved wrong made me feel like absolute crap for pushing Duckie to ask him in the first place. What kind of friend was I? "Oh, Duckie. I was so certain—"

"It would appear that you no longer have a date to the prom, Brooke. Because I'm going with Tucker." He raised his eyes to meet mine, a small smile on his lips.

It took a moment to register what he was saying. I was so relieved that I wasn't even mad. Putting my hands on his shoulders, I jumped off the stage and hugged him. He spun me around before setting me back on the stage with a grin. "Hey! Stop that or he'll get the impression I'm excited or something."

I couldn't stop smiling. "But you are."

"I so am." He hopped up to sit beside me. The teachers were still getting organized, so they wouldn't be ready for us for at least another ten minutes or so. Duckie leaned close so no one else would overhear. Not that anybody else was really paying attention to us. "It was perfect. I just asked him, and he said he'd been trying to figure out a way to ask me."

Sighing, I laid my head on Duckie's shoulder. Maybe there was some good in this world after all. "I love this moment. I want to freeze time for you right now, so you can stay here and feel all happy floaty."

"I don't want you to freeze time for me. Because if this moment is this good, what's coming up in the future?"

Duckie was such an optimist, even if he never wanted to admit it. Why on earth had he picked me to be his best friend?

I sat up straight and nudged him. "Your postprom kiss, for one."

"Oh my god! I totally forgot about that!" All the color drained out of his face, as if I'd just given him terrible news. It slowly returned, and when it did, his cheeks were blushing. "I may lose my mind. This is just so great. So crazy."

"Maybe you need a little crazy in your life." He definitely needed a little romance, that was for certain.

"Maybe you do too." He flashed me a knowing look. "Have you talked to Derek since his meltdown earlier?"

I pulled my phone out of my pocket and looked at the screen. Not one new text or call. "No."

People were starting to gather at the center of the gym, which meant that practice was on, and all things Derek would have to wait until later. We both hopped off the stage, and as we walked over to join the crowd, Duckie said, "I could swing you by his house on the way home after practice, if you want."

I bit my bottom lip in contemplation. "I don't know. Let me think about it."

And I did think about it. I thought about it all through the initial addressing of the crew. I thought about it as scripts were handed out and schedules were explained. I thought about it as the various speaking parts were introduced and applauded. I thought about it while I agreed to head up makeup crew once more. And during every other moment of our first rehearsal of the year.

An hour later, I hopped down from the stage and made my way to Duckie, who was engaged in what seemed like a really involved conversation with Tucker. He managed to tear his attention from Tucker for a moment, but I wasn't sure how long that would last. I said, "Hey, Duckman. Can I take you up on that offer to stop by Derek's on the way home?"

"No prob." And just like that, he turned back to Tucker. "So you're really related to David Bowie?"

Tucker nodded, his smile matching Duckie's. "Distantly, but yeah."

"I had such a crush on him in middle school. But hell, who didn't?" They both laughed after Duckie's quip, which made me wonder if Duckie had already forgotten about taking me to Derek's.

I tugged Duckie's sleeve. "Hey. Not to be a pain or anything, but do ya think we could go soon?"

Duckie stopped laughing. Yes, maybe I was being selfish about wanting to go see Derek. But he was the one who'd offered to take me.

Tucker said, "Hey, it's cool if you've gotta go. We can talk more tomorrow. Unless you want my number. Then we can text tonight. If you want."

They exchanged numbers and said their good-byes. All

the while an angry heat was coming from Duckie and aimed at yours truly. I deserved it.

After a too-quiet walk to the parking lot, we got into the Beast and took off. Not even ten minutes later, we'd pulled over and parked on the road outside Derek's house. The lights were on and Derek's dad's truck was nowhere to be seen. I didn't know how exactly to phrase it without Duckie eating me alive, but I still hadn't made up my mind about going to see Derek.

As calmly as possible, Duckie said, "Am I supposed to go in with you?"

"No." I could see someone moving around in the house and hoped it was Derek. Why wouldn't it be? His dad's truck was gone, and no one else lived there, as far as I knew. But I still had no idea what to say to him after the incident over my locker. *Thank you? That was kinda scary? Do you often defend people's honor, or is there something special between us?* My mind was whirling.

"Are you going to knock, or what?" Duckie sighed with a level of impatience that suggested I'd better make up my mind, and fast. Without further thought, I opened the door and got out, then shut the door and peeked through the window at Duckie for . . . I don't know. Wisdom, maybe? Support? With a forced smile, he started the Beast's engine again. "Good luck. I'm gonna head home.

Text me when you're ready to go."

I owed him the biggest apology, but it would have to wait.

My knees turned to Jell-O as I got closer to Derek's front porch. By the time I reached the door and knocked, I was fairly certain I was going to throw up.

The door opened, and Derek popped his head out to see who it was. To my relief, he smiled. "Oh, hey, Brooke. Come on in."

He stepped back, pushing the door open farther as an invitation. He was wearing nothing but a pair of jeans. As my eyes traced his torso, my mouth forgot how to speak. He grabbed a T-shirt from the back of the couch and slipped it on over his head. Which was a good thing. Otherwise the entire conversation would just be me ogling him.

When I stepped inside and could see his face better in the light, I realized that he had a black eye. His bottom lip was cut. I reached out to touch his face, but he shook me off, looking more embarrassed than anything. "Derek, oh my god, are you okay? I had no idea Eric hit you that hard."

"He didn't." His tone said that I should just drop it. Which meant that he had a lot to learn about me. "Hey, you want a sandwich or something?"

"No, thank you." I took his hand in mine and pulled him closer, keeping my eyes on his. "What happened?"

He swallowed hard and shrugged with one shoulder,

flitting his eyes about the room. "I got a three-day suspension and they sent me home. You sure you're not hungry?"

He was totally trying to change the subject, but I wasn't about to let him. "Derek . . . your eye . . ."

His jaw tightened, and a fearful look washed over him. After a moment of silence, during which he seemed to be debating what to tell me and how to tell it, he finally said, "That's just a little extra parenting from my old man after the school called and said to come pick me up. We got home and he let me have it. I knew it was coming, though, so it's no big deal."

No big deal. Right. "Are you okay?"

"I'm fine." He let go of my hand and leaned against the back of the couch.

Fine. He was fine. Yeah . . . so was I, even as the old man was pulling me out of Black River. I was fine. Utterly and completely fine, as far as I'd tell anyone. "Don't bullshit a bullshitter."

He wet his lips and met my gaze. "The truth?"

"Always."

"I'm not okay at all." I followed his attention to the pocketknife on the end table. His eyes welled with tears, but he quickly wiped them away. "I had the knife in my hand. I was seriously thinking about using it."

My heart sank at the idea of losing Derek. Was this what

it was like for people when they learned about my attempt?

"I'm glad you didn't."

"Why?" He looked at me, his eyes still shimmering. His bottom lip trembled slightly as he fought to keep from crying. The last thing I ever wanted to see was him hurting.

Stepping closer, I slipped my arms around his neck and gazed into his eyes. "Because you deserve better than being hurt. Especially by you."

He put his arms around me and pulled me closer, until my cheek was against his chest. I could hear his heart beating through the cotton of his shirt.

"Does your eye hurt?"

He sighed. "Yeah. But less now. My lip still stings, though."

"Too much for me to kiss you?" I pulled back just a bit so I could look at his face. Under his left eye, the skin was purple and slightly puffy. The cut on his lip looked as if it had been bleeding earlier, but had stopped. Even with his wounds, he was beautiful. I stood on my tiptoes and whispered, my lips close to his, "I can be gentle."

His breath was warm against my skin. "Please don't."

My heart started beating faster. He was so close, his chest against mine, our lips almost touching. I felt dizzy. "Don't kiss you?"

"No. Don't be gentle." He'd only just started to smile

when I pressed my lips against his. We kissed hard, and Derek tangled his fingers in my hair, pulling me as close as he could.

As our lips parted, I breathlessly asked, "So . . . where's your dad?"

Derek hesitated and then cocked an eyebrow at me. I could feel his heart racing. "He's . . . not in my bedroom."

People could say what they wanted about a woman's desire. They could slut-shame and insult women for having sex all they wanted. That didn't change the fact that having these feelings was normal . . . and pretty fantastic, if I was being honest.

I ran a finger down his nose to his lips and stopped at his chin. "Hmm. Maybe we should check just to be sure."

He took my hand in his and kissed my fingers before leading me to his room. The brief thought entered my mind that I'd only known him for roughly two weeks, but it passed quickly. I felt like I'd known him much longer than that. By the time we were inside his room and he'd closed the door, we were both smiling.

I took a seat on his bed, and the mattress sank in as he sat beside me, its springs creaking slightly beneath his weight. Our eyes met before mine fell to his mouth. I bit my bottom lip gently and raised my gaze to his eyes again. He leaned in, pressing his mouth to mine, kissing me. Our tongues slipped over each other, our lips moving with an increasing hunger. I felt his hand on my leg, where my knee-high socks ended and my skirt began. My skin flushed. It was exhilarating. It was terrifying. It felt wrong somehow, but oh so right.

I placed my right hand on the back of his head as we kissed, my fingers running through his hair. At the same time, I felt his fingers curl around the edge of one of my knee-high socks and pull it gently down my leg. It fell somewhere—I didn't care where—and then his fingers traced my skin. Goose bumps tickled up my calf, my thigh, as his hand moved upward. For a moment, a thin layer of panic washed over me. Was this what I wanted? Were we going too far? Too fast? As if sensing my hesitance, Derek broke our kiss gently and looked once more into my eyes. He whispered, "Is this okay?"

I didn't know if it was okay. I didn't know if I would regret it the next day or if things would change between us after this, or what I would do if I got pregnant or got a disease. My heart raced with questions and desire. I whispered back, "Do you have . . . something?"

He leaned over my lap and opened the drawer of his nightstand. Retrieving something, he closed the drawer and sat back, holding it up for me to see. It was a condom, which made me wonder how many girls he'd done this with before, or if he'd purchased them in preparation for getting me in his bed. Did he think I was easy? Did he think he could talk me into it if I wasn't interested? What went through a guy's mind on his way to the store to buy condoms, exactly? Other than the obvious.

As if sensing my doubt, Derek's cheeks flushed. "In case you're wondering, I only got them the other day. Just . . . just in case we ever . . . y'know. Have you ever . . . ?"

"Yeah. Twice. But those were . . . well . . . they were never . . . like this." My cheeks felt warm, and I knew that I must have been blushing. "What about you?"

"A couple of times." He looked serious for a moment and then placed a tiny peck on my forehead. "Nothing has to happen. Not if you don't want to. There are a million other things we can do together tonight. It's okay. Really."

I kissed him on the lips, lingering there in the tingle of his warmth.

When we parted, Derek seemed breathless. "What's that for?"

"For saying it's okay."

I kissed him again, a small moan escaping his mouth as I did, and his hand once again found my knee. Slowly, ever so slowly, his fingers inched up my thigh. As we lay back on the bed, his right hand found my hip. His mouth was hungry against mine, and it was all I could do not to devour him whole. Our bodies were pressed together, but I couldn't get close enough to him. He ground his hips into mine and I felt him against me—that hot, firm part of a guy that inspired whispers in the girls' locker room.

I'd had sex before, but both times it had been in the dark, and both times were awkward and over so quickly. Each experience had been about escapism, which was not at all what it was about with Derek. Derek made me want to be here, now. The thought crossed my mind that I loved him, but I tried to ignore it. Admitting that to myself could only open a doorway to pain. Besides, it was too soon for that. Wasn't it?

He pulled his body back momentarily, still kissing me. When our lips finally parted, he held my gaze and slipped his T-shirt off over his head, dropping it to the ground. His hands went slowly to his belt, undoing the buckle, then the button. As his fingers pulled the zipper of his jeans down, my heart fluttered in curiosity and fear. There was no going back now. And what's more, I didn't want to go back. What did that say about me? Was I a bad person? Was I a slut? Was this okay? If I were a guy, it would be fine, for some reason, by societal standards. So why did I feel bad for wanting to connect, to touch, to feel Derek's body against mine? Because I was female and we weren't supposed to want those things?

Shut up, brain, I thought as my eyes moved over his chest to his stomach.

He sat there on his knees, shirtless, jeans undone, watching me with smoldering eyes. Slowly, I slipped my shirt over my head and dropped it to the floor with his. As I lay back on the bed, he looked at me, his eyes tracing my curves. His voice was soft when he spoke and made my heart skip a beat. "You are so beautiful, Brooke. Just . . . perfect."

He bent down and kissed my neck, making a trail back to my mouth. His hand cupped my left breast momentarily and then it returned to my hip again, his fingers pulling my panties down and then off. My nails were digging gently into the smooth muscles of his shoulders. I felt like I was glowing, as if I might explode. His lips made his way to my ear, nibbling gently on my earlobe. He whispered, "Are you sure you're ready for this? We can stop."

In a breathy voice, I said, "No. I want to."

He sat back again, quickly removing his jeans. I averted my eyes. I couldn't look, couldn't see it just yet. It seemed so . . . absurdly personal to look at someone's private parts. Ridiculous, I know, considering what we were about to do. Considering that I'd had sex before. I had no idea if he planned to look at my parts or not, and honestly, I was too embarrassed to ask.

As he returned to me, my bra and skirt still on, I saw him drop the now-empty condom wrapper on the bed beside us. He kissed me deeply, and then I felt the heat and hardness of him against my thigh. Before I could breathe, he was slipping deep inside of me, and I moaned a little at the pain and pleasure and wonder of it all. My worry was gone for the moment, washed away by the push and pull of becoming one flesh, one soul. My body tingled in ways that it never had, and I was so glad that I was doing this with the boy I was completely in love with. And I did—oh god, I did love him. He was broken and imperfect and understood my soul. He was practically a stranger to me, and I didn't even know his last name. But I loved him. Good god, I loved him.

His skin smelled musky and manly. The bed creaked beneath us. Our hearts beat solidly together. One rhythm. One song.

Derek's hips began thrusting faster and faster until he called my name, his voice gruff and lost in complete ecstasy. As the quiet settled around us, he ran his fingers through my hair and whispered into my ear, his breath hot and trembling, "I love you."

And what's more, he meant it. I could feel it in his tone, in the way he looked at me, in his touch. Those words were better than any kiss, any touch that he had ever given me.

I smiled, feeling the warmth of him still inside of me, and said, "I love you too."

After he'd disposed of the condom, we snuggled for a long time. His body spooned up behind me, our skin touching, our warmth one. After a while—I wasn't sure how long—we dozed, tumbling deep into the sleep that can only come after such an intimate experience. I'd had sex before . . . but this was the first time that I'd ever made love. My lips curled into a smile as contented sleep dragged me under its waves.

When I opened my eyes, Derek was still behind me, holding me. He was so quiet, I was certain he was sleeping. The drapes were drawn, but it felt like night was still all around us. Beside the bed was a nightstand, but I didn't see a clock. I did see a copy of *Romeo and Juliet*, which gave me pause.

Derek spoke, his words hushed and gruff in my ear. I jumped a little at the sound of his voice. "You like Shakespeare?"

I rolled over so that I was facing him. His hair was mussed, his eyes bright. Reaching my hand up, I ran my fingers over the stubble on his chin. It was the first time I'd ever slept over with a guy. I wanted it to last. "Yeah. I mean, I actually can't stand *Romeo and Juliet*. Can I ask why you're reading it?"

He kissed my forehead and said, "Because I wanted to know more about what you and your friends were talking about."

My cheeks flushed. "That's incredibly sweet. But if you want to read Shakespeare, *Hamlet* was so much better."

"I don't know. There are some pretty great lines in *Romeo and Juliet*—most of them forgotten because of the overused ones. 'But, soft! what light through yonder window breaks? It is the east, and Juliet is the sun' is a pretty crappy line, if you think about it. But there are some good ones that no one seems to notice."

"So what are the good lines?"

He paused to think about it, but he didn't have to consider my question for long. "I like 'What is it else? A madness most discreet. A choking gall, and a preserving sweet.'"

I had no idea what he was talking about. "That's . . . nice? I guess. What does it mean exactly?"

"Basically?" He shrugged. "It means 'What is love? A sweet form of madness, a candy that you choke on.'"

"You're comparing love to madness. To craziness."

"So was Shakespeare." He ran a strand of my hair between his fingers and slowly swept it behind my left ear. "And there's not much of a difference, if you think about it. If it's real, I mean."

I blinked at him. "If what's real? The craziness or the love?"

"Both."

"How do you figure?"

"When someone's mad, truly mad, they lose control of themselves. They live in another state of mind—somewhere that you can only really understand if you've been there before." He shrugged. "It's the same way with love."

A question formed in my mind, but I was hesitant to ask it. I mean, he'd already answered it, I guessed, when he told me he loved me, but in that heated moment, people said all sorts of things. Didn't mean they meant it. I dropped my eyes and found the bravery to ask. "Have you ever been in love before?"

"Not until you." He smiled and placed a gentle kiss on my lips. "Y'know, just the presence of you makes me crazy. The absence of you too. It's dangerous and senseless . . . and beautiful."

It was the sweetest thing that anyone had ever said to me before. It couldn't be real. Could it? I so badly wanted it to be. A grin spread across my face. "You're just trying to get laid again."

His expression immediately turned serious. "I swear to you, if we never did it again, I'd be okay with that. Just . . . tell me that you love me. And I'll stay with you forever."

Forever. It sounded so perfect coming out of his mouth. I couldn't remember ever feeling so happy before. I met his gaze. "I love you."

He closed his eyes as if relishing the moment. When he looked at me again, he sighed. "Now comes the bad news."

My heart paused in fear. "What's that?"

Derek kissed my neck, leaving a trail of pecks along my shoulder. "We have to get you home before your parents realize you slept here."

"Shit! What time is it?" I practically leapt from the bed, throwing on my clothes as fast as I possibly could.

Derek just lay there, watching me. The blanket was only covering him from the waist down. "It's almost six in the morning. School starts in an hour."

"Shit. Okay. I'll text Duckie. Where's my phone?"

"I don't remember seeing it last night."

Great. Not only did I fail to check in with my parents last night, but now I'd lost my phone. They were going to ground me until I was twenty.

As I slid my knee-high socks back on, I tilted my head at Derek in wonder. "Won't your dad notice me sneaking out of your bedroom?"

He shook his head and grabbed his boxers from the foot of the bed. The temptation to peek at him as he got dressed filled me, and I didn't bother resisting. As he slipped into his jeans, he said, "I sincerely doubt he even made it home from the bar last night. He usually crashes at a buddy's or in his truck in the bar parking lot."

His family life was so completely different from mine. I couldn't imagine my dad going to a bar, let alone not coming home from one that night. "Has he always been like that?"

"Yeah. For as long as I can remember, anyway." He zipped up his jeans and pulled his T-shirt on over his head. We looked pretty much as we had the night before. But something was different now. We were bonded in a very special way—almost like we shared a secret. Well, it was a secret now. It would remain one until I told Duckie, of course. Derek handed me my left shoe and said, "My mom was a druggie who ditched me with my grandparents till I was ten. Then after they died, there was nowhere else for me to go but with my dad."

"Is he always—"

"An asshole? Yeah. Yeah, he is." Briefly, a pained look crossed his features, but it faded when he met my eyes. "But's no big deal."

Except that it was, and it was written all over his face.

Derek handed me his phone, and I texted Duckie. It wasn't long before he turned into the driveway. Before I stepped off the porch, Derek caught my elbow in his hand and pulled me back to him. "Love me?"

I smiled, stood on my tiptoes, and placed a gentle peck on his forehead. "Love you."

As I slid into the passenger's seat, I said, "I am the worst friend in the world and totally stepped over the line in the most selfish way possible by tearing you away from Tucker last night, and I'm sorry."

Duckie sat there silent for a moment. Then he put the car in gear. "Apology accepted. By the way, I found your phone in the Beast when I got home. And then I pretended to be you when your mom texted to check on you last night. Just so you know, you had a lovely time playing dirty Scrabble with me. You only won because you cheated."

He held up my phone, and I took it from him with a smile. Duckie was the best.

"Also . . . you had sex. And I want to hear every sweaty detail."

I turned my head toward him, "How did you know?"

"I didn't." He glanced my way over the top of his round sunglasses. "You just told me."

CHAPTER TWELVE

"Boardwalk is mine. You're goin' down, doc." I moved my little thimble gentleman onto the coveted blue property and held out my hand.

"Don't be so sure. You underestimate the value of well-placed hotels on cheap properties." He handed me the property card. He sounded pretty sure of himself, despite the fact that I also owned Park Place. At least I was getting better at playing Monopoly. That much he couldn't deny. "So how are you, Brooke?"

Five sessions in, I'd finally come to the conclusion that I liked the doc. Talking about stuff was still difficult, but it was getting easier. Much easier on this day—a day there would be no tears or pain. "Weirdly, I'm really happy, doc. Makeup crew's been going well the past few weeks. My grades are getting better—well, except for AP History, but let's not open that wound. And I've decided I truly actually like folding origami cranes. The whole process of paper folding is cool. I checked out a few books on origami. Might try something more complex soon, y'know?"

He nodded and rolled the dice, a contemplative look on his face. He got a six and started moving his race car across the board. "That all sounds great. It's nice to hear you're getting out there and moving forward. Are the cranes helping?"

"When I first started folding them at home, I thought a lot about Joy. Remember? The girl who killed herself while I was inpatient?" I raised an eyebrow at Dr. Daniels and he nodded in response. I didn't usually talk about Joy. But today I could. Today was different. It was an up day. "I thought about how the inpatient staff all gave us these cheesy ideas about how to save our own lives by folding birds out of paper and how it wasn't enough for her. I really resented them for that. They told us to use origami as a distraction from our suicidal thoughts. When I started making them at home, I'd make one every time I thought about dying. I have hundreds now. They hang over my bed."

The race car came to a stop on Free Parking, so the doc

collected the four-hundred-dollar pot from the middle of the board with a smile. Then he handed me the dice. "Are you concerned at all that you might be feeding your urges to harm yourself? Are they a reminder of your suicide attempt?"

Shaking my head, I dropped the dice on the board. "Not anymore. I'm making them for a different reason now."

"And what's that?"

I moved two spaces and cursed under my breath. It never failed. Every single time I landed on a space between Go and Jail, I ended up paying rent to the doc. "I fold an origami crane every time I think of a reason to live. Even if some of those reasons might seem like the same reason."

"What do you mean?" He looked at me thoughtfully and reached for the dice. Almost as an afterthought, he said, "You owe me rent, by the way. I told you those cheaper properties can be sneaky."

As I forked over the cash, I said, "That interesting guy I told you about almost a month ago? His name is Derek. And I'm making cranes because of him now. One crane is for the way he smirks. One is for the color of his eyes. One is for the way my breath catches when he looks at me."

It sounded ridiculously cheesy and vomit inducing, but I couldn't help it. Derek was the love of my life.

The doc paused noticeably before speaking again. "I see. Are you two close?"

"Really close. I love him. Sometimes I feel like he's the only person who really understands me." *Sorry, doc.* "When I was in the hospital, the doctors said I needed to find my reason to live."

"And?"

Smiling, I met his eyes. I hadn't felt this light, this in control, this happy in a long time. "Well, I have. Derek is my reason."

Dr. Daniels set the dice on the table without rolling them. He leaned forward and spoke slowly and crisply in order to drive his point home. His left ring finger was bare. "You need to be careful, Brooke. Careful not to put too much of your will to live on the shoulders of another person. I'm pleased that your reasons for making the cranes have changed, and that Derek has inspired this newfound hope in you. But sooner or later, you're going to have to learn to live for yourself."

My alarm clock flashed 2:52 a.m., and I groaned. I couldn't sleep. I was too mad to sleep. Mad at the doc for saying what he'd said about Derek. What was so wrong with loving someone so much that they gave you a reason to keep living?

How could he insinuate that that was a bad thing? Just when I was finally starting to kinda like the doc, he had to go and say something insensitive. Figured.

Lurking beneath my anger was a question that I didn't want to ask. I rolled over so that I didn't have to see my alarm clock anymore and curled into a ball. The question poked and prodded at the back of my mind, demanding to be heard.

What if the doc was right?

I sat up and threw my quilt off, willing the question to vanish into the night air. Then I stood up and went downstairs. Maybe some milk would help me sleep.

When I reached the bottom of the stairs, I noticed the light in the kitchen was on. I rounded the corner and found my dad standing in front of the open refrigerator. Apparently I wasn't the only one experiencing a bit of insomnia. I cleared my throat so he'd know I was in the room. The last thing I needed was to give my dad a heart attack by coming up behind him in the middle of the night and saying hi.

He turned around, surprised that he wasn't alone in the kitchen at almost three in the morning, and said, "Caught in the act. What's it gonna be? Jail? Making small rocks into smaller rocks?"

I smiled. "I think I can let you off with a warning this time. Can't sleep?"

Dad's shoulders slumped. "Not a wink. I was hoping to

find company in the fridge. Maybe in the form of leftovers."

I sat at the counter and said, "Mom baked brownies earlier."

"That'll work." He retrieved two glasses and filled them both with milk as I removed the lid from the plastic container. As he picked up a double-fudge brownie, he said, "What's got you up so late? Or early, I guess."

"My brain won't shut up." A sigh escaped me. It was nice to have Dad's ear again—if only for a moment. The truth was, I'd missed our talks. "Dad, have you ever felt like you're totally right about something, but then had someone come in and stomp all over your rightness?"

"Of course." He spoke through a mouthful of chocolate. "Know what I do in that situation?"

"What's that?"

He pointed his half-eaten brownie at me. I liked seeing him this way—loving, kind. Not the quiet, angry man who hid behind his newspaper and avoided eye contact with me. "I trust my gut. Usually it's right. Sometimes it's not. But on those rare occasions when my gut feeling is wrong, I take what lessons I can from the experience and move forward."

My gut said that Dr. Daniels was wrong about me relying on Derek as a reason to keep going. It also said that I should eat the brownie in my hand before my stomach started to rumble with hunger. "How'd you get so smart?"

Dad smiled and held his glass up to me in a toasting gesture before taking a drink. "I listened to your grandma for forty-three years."

He'd always said that I reminded him of Grandma. When I'd looked at pictures of her from when she was younger, I could see an uncanny resemblance. But more than that, before Grandma died, she was the person I'd felt closest to. Maybe that was because we were so alike. I wasn't sure. But one thing I did know: if this advice was coming from Grandma, it was solid.

I took a bite and chewed, suddenly grateful for my parents. "So what's got *you* up in the middle of the night?"

Dad looked at me, apparently not sure how to answer. "Just . . . worrying."

Polishing off my midnight snack, I thought about how alike my dad and grandma had been. Did that mean that he and I were alike as well? Maybe. "What about?"

"Everything. Work. Your mother. You."

"Well, you don't need to worry about me. I'm actually doing really well." And I was. Honestly.

He nodded, curious. "How's that head shrink treating you?"

Remembering the doc's final words from our latest session, I broke my brownie in two. "He's okay. I think he cheats at Monopoly, though."

Dad looked at me blankly. "Well, have you tried buying up all the cheap properties and putting hotels on them? It's amazing how much people underestimate a strategy like that."

I very nearly face-palmed. Was everyone better at Monopoly than me? At life? "I think I'm going to try to get some sleep. You staying up to worry some more?"

He paused and then gave me a half smile. "I guess I'll give it a rest for a night. Sweet dreams, kiddo."

On the counter was a small stack of papers, tastefully organized and stapled together. It looked like one of Dad's out-of-town work itineraries. "Wait. What's this?"

He rinsed his glass and set it in the sink with a sigh. "It's for a business trip that the execs and their spouses were supposed to attend. But I'm canceling it. We should be home with you. So it's nothing, really."

"Dad, you really don't have to worry about leaving me alone. I'm doing much better now." He didn't look very convinced. "What if Duckie stayed the weekend with me? It's just two days. Come on. Give me a chance to show you how much better I'm doing."

He eyed me for a second, glanced at the itinerary, and then eyed me some more. Then he picked up his plate, set it next to his glass in the sink, and shook his head. "Your mother is going to throw a fit."

"Let her throw a fit. Maybe it'll be good for her." I gave him a smile, glad that he was starting to trust me again, relieved that we were talking.

As Dad walked out of the room, he planted a kiss on top of my head and chuckled. "That's just what your grandma would've said."

CHAPTER THIRTEEN

When the alarm went off at six, I wanted to throw it across the room, but I managed to resist the urge. I turned it off and dragged myself through my morning routine. By the time Duckie rolled up in the Beast, I was clean and dressed, but half-asleep. It was a wonder I remembered to take my meds and grab my backpack on the way out the door. I opened the door of the Beast and oozed into the seat. Duckie laughed. "Rough night, princess?"

I hated when he called me that. He'd only done it maybe four times in our entire friendship, but each time incited a glare from me. "Something like that, yeah. I only slept for maybe two and a half hours. Today is going to last so long."

"Even longer than you think, I'm betting." He glanced at me and said, "Did you forget we have rehearsal tonight?"

"Ugh." I slumped down in my seat, exhausted. "Y'know, after six years of being in theater, I still don't get why it's all hands on deck for every practice. They don't do that at any other school. It's so stupid. Most of us just end up standing around all night, waiting to go home."

Duckie rolled his eyes as he navigated our way to school. "Oh, please. You love it and you know it. Being surrounded by like minds. Watching the play come together like a complex puzzle. They want all hands on deck at every practice so that we each can learn and appreciate all the hard work that it takes to make a play happen."

It took every fiber of my being to hold my tongue. I was too tired to listen to Duckie go on about details I already knew. I'd just wanted somebody to agree with me for the moment, until I'd slept more and felt better about everything. I lay my head against the door. "I'm gonna doze."

Duckie's voice was almost too perky for me to handle. "When you wake up, be less grumpy, okay?"

I didn't actually think I'd fall asleep on the short drive to school, but I realized I had when the Beast backfired and my heart nearly jumped out of my chest. Duckie laughed and said, "Good morning. Again. Less grumpy now?"

"No." My tone was biting and I knew it, but didn't much care. I opened the door and reluctantly pulled myself from the Beast.

As I stood next to it, trying to ready myself for the day, Duckie walked around the front and handed me my backpack, which I'd apparently left inside. Snatching it out of his hands, I grumbled my gratitude. He glanced behind me and said under his breath, "Maybe this will help."

Now all-too-familiar hands slid around my waist, and Derek's voice filled my ear. "Hey. I missed you. Why didn't you text me back?"

"You texted me?" I pulled my phone out of my pocket and looked at the screen. Seven missed texts from Derek. "Oh, I'm sorry. I was up really late and distracted. I must not have heard my phone."

"Up late? Where were you, some party?" He gave my neck a little kiss, and I couldn't help but smile at his sweetness.

"No, I was home. But my stupid therapist said something that wouldn't let me sleep, so I was tossing and turning all night."

"That sucks." I turned around in his arms and kissed his still-injured lip lightly. His eyes were full of concern. "I was worried."

What was this? Worry-about-Brooke week?

Duckie was right. I was super grumpy.

Shaking my head, I said, "I'm sorry. There's nothing to worry about."

Derek planted a kiss on my forehead and we started walking toward the school, hand in hand. Duckie picked up his pace and moved ahead of us, making himself scarce. He'd been doing that a lot the past few weeks whenever Derek was around.

Derek said, "I was thinking we should hang out tonight. Maybe catch a movie or something?"

We moved up the front steps toward the door. Miller was standing just outside, trying to strike fear into the hearts of several hundred teenagers who couldn't give a crap about him. I shook my head at Derek. "I can't tonight. I have rehearsal and I'm so tired, I could probably fall asleep standing up right now. Maybe this weekend?"

"Maybe?" He stopped walking, pulling his hand from mine.

When I turned around, I could see that I'd hurt his feelings without meaning to. "Hey. You okay?"

The air between us lightened almost immediately.

"Yeah. I just had a bad night too." He pulled me closer and whispered in my ear, "Still love me?"

My heart felt like it might burst. It was the first good thing to happen today. "Absolutely."

He reached up with both hands and gripped the collar of

my jacket, smiling. His tone was commanding. "Say it."

"I love you." My legs felt weak, and my mind insisted on bringing up images from Derek's bedroom a few days before.

"I love you too." Derek smiled and leaned in, kissing me hard on the mouth. As we parted, I could see Miller huffing his way toward us out of the corner of my eye. "You sure you can't ditch rehearsal?"

Guilt gnawed on my insides until I said, "Okay. One movie and then I've gotta get some sleep, okay?"

Derek grinned. "Okay."

As we walked toward the school, Miller was distracted by a small scuffle, which set my mind at ease. The last thing I needed today was Miller. "So what movie are we seeing?"

Derek opened the door and held it for me. As I stepped inside, he said, "Who cares? I planned to kiss you all through it anyway."

It was sweet. And it should have been endearing. But with my lack of sleep, it felt a bit pointless—something I attributed to my bad mood.

The rest of the day flew by in a blur. Probably because I took at least one short nap each class period. It was practically a miracle that I managed to survive the day at school, get home, and finish a paper for economics class on some Scottish philosopher named Adam Smith before dashing out the door at the sound of the Beast's engine. I slid into the passenger's seat, and Duckie backed out of the driveway without a word. It was almost like he could sense what I was about to say.

"So . . . I kinda told Derek I'd go to a movie with him tonight. Would you mind covering for me if anyone asks where I am?"

"I suppose you want me to drop you at his house, then?"

"Yeah. If that's okay with you."

Duckie didn't say whether or not it was okay with him, and I didn't ask, because judging by his tone, we both knew that it wasn't. All I could do was try to reassure him that practice would go on fine without me. "The play is really starting to come together, isn't it? I mean, a few of the actors still aren't off book, but the sets are built enough that the gym is looking less like the gym and more like Verona. Don't you think?"

He made a sound, but didn't respond otherwise. So much for reassuring him.

As Duckie pulled into Derek's driveway, he said, "See you tomorrow, princess."

I groaned. "Duckie, I'm sorry. I know I've been really grumpy and dismissive today. And I know it's pretty crappy of me to ditch rehearsal tonight, but Derek really wants to be with me right now. You might think I'm the worst friend ever, but I'm sorry . . . I have to do this."

He smiled, but it didn't seem genuine. "It's okay. You just go enjoy your date."

We locked eyes for a moment. And in that silent conversation, I pleaded with Duckie to try to understand. But he tore his gaze away before I could get confirmation that he did. I exited the Beast and made my way to the front door before I realized that I hadn't told Duckie "I-L-Y." When I turned back to the car, he was holding up one hand in the "I love you" ASL gesture. With a small, apologetic smile, I returned the favor and knocked on the front door.

The door opened just as the Beast was pulling away, and Derek greeted me with a kiss. As we parted, his brow furrowed. "Everything okay?"

I wanted it to be but hated the way I'd left things with the Duckman. Still, not wanting to ruin the evening, I shook it off and said, "Just peachy. So . . . how are we getting to the movies exactly?"

Vikas was stretched out on the couch, half-asleep. When he opened his eyes briefly and saw me, he wagged his tail some before settling back into a nice doggy slumber.

Holding a finger up, Derek disappeared into his bedroom for a moment before returning with two motorcycle helmets. Handing me the smaller one, which had a skull on each side, he said, "My dad's gone for the night, so we're taking his bike."

Ignoring the fact that I'd had no idea his dad even had a motorcycle—and the fact that I was pretty sure if I got on it, I'd probably have my brains splattered all over the pavement by night's end—I said, "Aren't you worried you'll get in trouble?"

"Nah. He left the shed unlocked and the key in the ignition, so it's kinda his fault anyway. I'll have it back before he ever knows, so we're good. You ready?"

Every cell in my body, every nerve ending in my skin, every synapse in my brain said that I was certainly *not* ready to get on a motorcycle for the first time. Not now, probably not ever. "I . . . don't know about this, Derek."

"What's the matter?" He slipped his helmet on and began to buckle the strap under his chin. Then he gave me a wink. "You're not scared, are you?"

Scared? No. Not me. *Terrified* would have been a much more appropriate word to describe how I was feeling at that moment. But as frightened as I was of the prospect of whipping down roads with no metal cage to protect me, I was more worried about the idea of disappointing my boyfriend.

With trembling hands, I slipped my helmet on and said,

"You'll have to help me with the strap. I . . . I've never actually done this before."

Derek didn't look surprised. He also didn't look judgmental. As he did up my chin strap, he explained, "No big deal. Just remember that the key to being a good passenger is to learn how to lean and relax into the seat. Let me do the navigating. You just sit back and enjoy the ride."

He led me out the front door and around the house to a small shed. When he opened the door and pulled a string, a single lightbulb lit up the small space. The shed was only big enough for a couple toolboxes and the bike, but I immediately saw why his dad normally had it locked. The motorcycle was in pristine condition, in complete contrast to every other item they owned. The machine seemed so foreign to its surroundings that my eyes were drawn immediately to it. It had been painted in shimmering pewter and burgundy, and had so much chrome that I actually wondered how long it took to polish it to a shine. Before I realized it, Derek had taken a seat on the leather and, after putting up the kickstand, pushed the bike out of the shed. He turned his head to me and said, "Hop on. Just make sure you get on from the left side, so you don't burn yourself on the pipes. They can get pretty hot."

My heart was in my throat. What was I doing? Putting my life in danger just to impress a guy?

Derek met my eyes. "We don't have to take a ride if you're not okay with it."

"No. I'm okay." Pushing down every last bit of anxiety in my stomach, I climbed up behind him and sat down. Because this wasn't just a guy. It was Derek.

Once he put the bike in neutral, he turned the key and hit the start button. The engine rumbled to life, shaking beneath me, matching the flutter in my chest. He pulled back on the throttle, and the engine growled. It sounded like the machine was a wild animal that had just been set free from its cage. He leaned back a bit and said, "Just relax and try to enjoy it. You ready?"

Everything in my brain screamed *no*, but my mouth opened and I said, "Yes."

Before I knew it, the bike was in gear and we were moving forward. Derek rode down the driveway and turned onto the road. I gripped his shirt in my hands, prepared to scream in terror.

Only . . . it wasn't terrifying. It was exhilarating. As the speedometer climbed, my stomach filled with the same kind of tickly sensation that I got whenever I rode a roller coaster and went over a hill. I relaxed back in my seat and put my hands behind me, holding on to the bars of the seat back rather than clutching on to Derek in fear. The lack of metal around me opened up the entire world to me. I'd had no idea how much of it was concealed by riding inside a car. The sky looked bigger somehow, and the trees, the buildings, even the stars looked more real, more . . . defined. Every time Derek revved the engine and sped up, I found myself laughing. As we pulled to a stop at the corner where we needed to turn to head for the movie theater, Derek leaned back and said, "Turn and see a movie, or keep going?"

Grinning, I said, "Don't stop! Keep going!"

He did a fast takeoff, and I felt something that I hadn't in a long time. I felt free.

We rode around for a couple of hours, enjoying the scenery, the smells, the breeze, before Derek navigated us toward his house. As we approached his driveway, he reached back with his left hand and gave my leg a gentle squeeze. Once we got to the shed, he paused and told me to hop off. After I did, he backed the bike into the shed and parked it exactly as it had been before putting the kickstand down and shutting off the engine. He climbed off and turned off the light, then came out, shutting the doors behind him. I was still grinning, but struggling to undo my chin strap. Derek removed his helmet and then gently unsnapped the strap for me before placing a peck on the tip of my nose. "Did you have fun?"

"Much more than I expected. When can we go again?" I pulled the helmet off and shook my hair loose.

Smiling, he shook his head. "That all depends. Dad doesn't forget his bike key often, and there's no way he'd ever give me permission to ride her."

"Why not? You seem to know what you're doing."

A sad glint entered Derek's eyes. "That bike is the only thing he's kept that reminds him of my mom. They used to ride together a lot. Y'know. Before."

I didn't know, but I nodded anyway.

He shook off whatever memories had been invoked by our ride and said, "Anyway. I'm glad you had fun. Want me to walk you home?"

"I'd love that. But I just realized . . . my parents think I'm coming back home in Duckie's car. How am I going to explain walking?"

Shrugging, he said, "Just tell them the car was getting low on gas, so he dropped you at the corner."

I decided that wasn't completely implausible. The Beast did have a tendency to guzzle fuel. "Okay. But you have to kiss me good-bye before we get to my house. If they see you, I'm as good as grounded."

The corner of his mouth lifted in a sly smile. "I love it when you get commanding."

As promised, Derek kissed me good night well out of range of my house. At first, it was tender, but then he slid his hands around my waist. His tongue flicked over mine with a hint of hunger. I gently pushed him away. "I wish we could keep doing this, but if I don't get inside soon, they'll be suspicious."

His eyes slowly scanned my face, my neck, and as they lowered, I saw in his gaze the same hunger that had been in his kiss. "Y'know, my dad's gonna be gone all night."

I kissed his lips and pulled farther away. "Not tonight. Now go home and take care of Vikas. I'm sure he's lonely."

After a long pause, Derek chuckled. "There's that commanding tone I love so much."

I squeezed his hand and let our fingers graze against one another as we parted and I moved away. "Good night. I love you."

"I love you more."

I rolled my eyes before giving him a wink. "As if."

Lucky for me, Mom and Dad totally bought my story, and the evening progressed without a hitch. But as the adrenaline of our ride eased off, my lack of sleep started catching up to me. After I nearly fell asleep in my bowl of take-out chili, my parents insisted I go upstairs and get to bed. I went without argument. As soon as my head hit the pillow, darkness consumed me and I drifted there for hours. I was so deep under that I thought it was a dream when I felt my bed move. But I woke enough to see a shape in the night, a person, in my room, on my bed. I opened my mouth to scream.

A warm hand covered my mouth, and I heard Derek whisper, "Shh. It's just me."

Pushing his hand away, I sat up, still flustered. "Derek? What are you doing here? How did you get in?"

He sat back on the bed, looking a bit deflated. "Your bedroom window was unlocked. I wanted to surprise you."

"Well, it worked." I put my hand to my chest. My heart was racing with fear. I might have been tired all day, but I was for sure awake now.

Derek caressed my arm. "I'm sorry I scared you. I thought it would be romantic."

"To break into my house and scare the shit out of me?"

"Well, not when you say it like that." He shook his head as the realization hit him that he hadn't quite thought this out before acting. "Jesus, that makes me sound like such a creeper. I am so sorry. You want me to go?"

"You kinda have to. You can't stay. My parents would freak."

"What if I leave before the sun comes up?" He scooted closer and kissed my neck. Happy tingles flowed through me.

I pushed him away with a chuckle. "We are not having sex."

"I didn't come here for sex. I came here because . . . I should just go. I'm sorry." His shoulders sank.

He started to stand, but I grabbed his arm and pulled

him gently back onto the bed. "No, stay. But you have to promise to leave in an hour, okay? If I get caught with a guy in my room, let alone in bed with me, my parents will—"

"I get it. One hour. I promise." We both lay down and he curled up behind me, spooning me. Brushing my hair away from my face, he kissed along my jawline and whispered, "I really am sorry I scared you. It was a stupid idea."

Understatement of the year. "That's okay."

I said that, but it didn't feel okay. Derek's body snuggled up behind me felt wonderful. As did his fingers playing with strands of my hair. As did his lips pressed against the back of my neck in the occasional little kiss.

But it felt weird to know that someone—even if it was my boyfriend—had crawled through my bedroom window in the middle of the night and gotten into bed with me without my noticing. I was probably blowing it out of proportion, but I made a mental note to lock my window at night from here on out.

I dozed off with Derek's strong arms around me, which made me feel safe. True to his promise, an hour later, he kissed my cheek and crawled back out my window without a word. He probably thought I was sleeping. After he left, I did sleep, but my dreams were troubled.

CHAPTER FOURTEEN

"Wow. What a creeper." Duckie had a sharp eyebrow raised as he brought the Beast to a stop in the school's parking lot. He turned off the ignition and took the key out with an air of disgust.

"He's not a creeper. He just wasn't thinking, I guess." It sounded like such a creeper move to break into my room at night and crawl into bed with me, so how could I defend his actions? "He said he thought it would be romantic."

Duckie gave me a look laced with disbelief and grabbed his messenger bag before getting out the driver's side door. "Well, I guess he can't be pretty *and* smart."

"Listen. Don't tell Derek I told you about last night, okay? I don't want him to think—" Suddenly my mind went blank. "I don't know. Just don't say anything."

Duckie furrowed his brow at me as I exited the car.

"Why would you assume that I'd say anything, Brooke? I'm hurt. Really." Just as he noticed Derek's approach, he muttered so that only I would hear, "Oh, look, the creeper's here . . ."

"Duckie!" My heart was in my throat.

Duckie shook his head and walked away. "Sorry, can't talk now. Busy, busy, busy."

Derek watched him, looking more than a little embarrassed. When he looked back at me, his face was flushed. "You told him about last night, didn't you?"

"He's my best friend. I tell him everything." All I could do was cringe and make plans to strangle Duckie later. "Sorry."

"Don't worry about it. He's right. What I did was way out of line. I feel terrible." His shoulders were slumped and he seemed to be having a difficult time meeting my eyes.

The majority of our classmates were already inside, or walking up the front steps. If we didn't get moving, Miller was going to give us an earful. But this was important.

Tugging lightly on Derek's sleeve, I said, "Just . . . text me first next time, okay?"

He gave me a wink. "Come on. It never bothered you before."

My heart skipped a nervous beat. "Wh—"

Derek chuckled and pulled me into his arms before placing a kiss on my forehead. "Kidding. I'm just kidding."

I laughed softly, but it didn't quite fill me with relief. Of course he was kidding. Derek would never do something like that. I mean, besides last night . . .

The first half of my day flew by, and my classes weren't nearly as bad as I thought they'd be. Hell, even Mr. Rober's class was semi-bearable. Duckie was really quiet the few times I saw him, but I assumed he was just tired or something.

Come lunchtime, Duckie was leaning against the wall to the left of the cafeteria doors as I approached, looking sullen. "Hey. You okay?"

He shook his head. "What are you doing, Brooke?"

I stumbled over my response. "Going . . . to lunch?"

"I mean, what are you doing with Derek? You guys got super serious super fast, and after the guy totally breaks into your house, into your *bedroom*"—he put such emphasis on the word that it sounded sinister, ugly—"you defend him and go on acting like this is all normal. It's not."

"I—"

"Not to mention that you've never treated me like I was a second thought until the creeper came along." The pain he was feeling was evident in his expression. Pain that I had caused. Pain that I never wanted him to feel.

"I'm sorry, Duckie. I just . . . love him." It was a poor excuse for an apology, and I knew it. But I didn't know what else to say.

"You can't love him after only a month. You can like him, lust after him, but love takes time." He was being Serious Duckie again. "I'm worried about you. And I'm not sure this guy is good for you. Just . . . just be careful, okay?"

A part of me wondered if maybe my best friend was right. But another part said that he didn't understand. And I needed him to understand. "Look, I know that things between Derek and me have been moving really fast. And you're right. I should probably slow things down and examine my feelings. But Duckie, I've never felt this way before. He's my first thought in the morning and my last thought at night. So what else could it be besides love?"

He tilted his head back, closing his eyes, and sighed like he was trying to gather some strength. "I have to tell you something."

Breathless, I said, "About Derek?"

"No. It's definitely not about Derek. There are other people in the world." When he looked at me again, his cheeks were slightly pink. "I have news. Good news, actually. Really good news."

"Tell me."

He grabbed me by the shoulders and said, "Tucker kissed me. In the hall. Right after drama club."

"Shut up!" I jumped up and smacked him on the arm in shock and joy and awe. His dream guy finally kissed him. It was amazing. For the first time in our history, Duckie and I were both in relationships at the same time. At least, I presumed. Tucker didn't seem like the kind of guy to kiss and ditch. But then, what did I know?

He was beaming at last. "Make up your mind. Do you want me to tell you about it or shut up?"

My heart felt so full of joy for him. He was going to be okay. Better than okay. Duckie was going to be happy. "I need details. Now. Does this mean you're boyfriends?"

"Well, rather than give you details in short bursts throughout the day, why don't I come over tonight and we can watch *Pretty in Pink* and talk all through Blaine's dialogue?"

"That sounds amazing. We haven't watched it in months. Let's do it." I wrapped my arm around his and as we headed back to the lunchroom, I marveled at how much our lives had changed in the months since my suicide attempt. Things had been so bleak back then, so hard—for both of us. But they seemed to be improving. Man, I hoped so. "I can't believe he kissed you!"

He raised an eyebrow at me, a smirk on his lips. "Are you

saying that there exists a person somewhere on this planet who's capable of resisting my indefinable charm?"

I gave his arm a squeeze. "Not a one, Duckie. Not a one."

As we took our seats at our usual table, Derek approached and set his tray down. He took the seat next to mine and smiled. I could feel Duckie bristle at his presence. Derek said, "So, there's no school tomorrow because of that teachers' in-service thing. Do you wanna do something together tonight?"

"I can't. Sorry. Can we do it tomorrow? I kinda made plans with Duckie."

"Oh." His eyebrows came together momentarily, but he quickly relaxed and shrugged it off. "That's cool. We can get together tomorrow, if you want."

"You are awesome. Tomorrow it is." With a peck on his cheek, the subject was closed. Could I really have it all? A life? With a terrific boyfriend and an amazing best friend? No razors, no plan? Just hope for a bright future. Was it possible?

That strange sense of lightness carried me through the rest of the day, and I wondered if it was all due to Derek or if the meds were actually doing something. I didn't feel like I was medicated. There was no mental fog or weird drugged feeling. I just felt . . . better, somehow. Not perfect, but better.

That night at the dinner table, Dad and I were thumb-wrestling while Mom set a bowl of salad on the table. He was winning, but the salad effectively ended our match. We exchanged looks of wonder when she followed it up with a tray that held a roast and cooked veggies. As she sat down, Dad and I just looked at her. Finally noticing our disbelieving stares, she said, "What?"

"You . . . you cooked?" I tried not to sound so shocked, but my mother—the queen of takeout—did not cook roasts or make salads. So clearly something was up.

"I just thought I'd give cooking a try. So I pulled out your grandmother's recipe book and gave it a shot. Would you rather we order a pizza?"

Dad reached across the table and gave her hand a squeeze. "It smells delicious. You're just full of surprises, that's all."

Mom relaxed, and we filled our plates. Dad had been right about the yummy smells, and the taste put even those to shame. After a while, Mom said, "There is another reason I cooked. I thought it would be nice to celebrate how well you're doing lately, Brooke."

A smile touched my lips. "Mom, you didn't have to do that. But thank you."

Dad wiped his mouth with his napkin and said, "Your mother and I are very proud of you, kiddo. There's been a big change in you lately. You seem happier."

"I am happier." My mind immediately turned to Derek. I hadn't told my parents that we were dating. Not yet. What if I told them and they didn't like the idea of me dating him? Mom hadn't exactly looked impressed when she'd met him.

My stomach churned with guilt, and I was relieved when the subject turned to Dad's plans for the evening. Even though Mom was super reluctant. "Drinks and dancing? I thought we'd have a nice night in."

"We've had enough nights in lately. Let's go out and have some fun." He flashed her a look full of unspoken words—words she apparently understood.

"All right. But Brooke, you and Ronald had better behave yourselves while we're out."

Dad said, "Ronald's coming over? You know it's a school night, right?"

I swallowed the bite in my mouth and said, "We have tomorrow off. Teachers' in-service day or something."

The doorbell rang, and I stood, pushing my chair back from the table. "Speak of the Duckie."

An hour later, Duckie and I had finished washing, drying, and putting away the dishes. Mom and Dad had gotten dressed to go out, and as they shut the front door behind them, Duckie and I did a little happy dance. Once their car was out of the driveway, we grabbed snacks from the kitchen and readied ourselves for a parent-free evening. Up in my room, I considered telling him that I thought my medication might be making a difference after all, but I didn't want to overshadow his happy gossip. I'd tell him another time.

"It was perfect." Duckie had a giant bowl of buttered popcorn in his arms. He set it on the bed, and I handed him one of the cans of soda I'd been carrying. "We were talking about how Mercutio and Benvolio are some of the best characters in the play, and I was explaining why I thought Benvolio was a better friend to Romeo than Mercutio."

"You are such a theater geek." I set my soda on my dresser and started making a pile of pillows on the floor at the foot of my bed. When we had *Pretty in Pink* nights, it was all about comfort.

"Says the other theater geek in the room." Duckie sat on the floor and leaned back against the huge pillow pile. "Anyway. I thought it was kinda weird, because we've been working on the play this whole time and our conversations have pretty much covered all things *Romeo and Juliet* related. Lately, we've been talking about other stuff. Goals, dreams. Bigger stuff. So I started wondering if maybe he was pulling back, y'know? Like maybe he'd decided that I just wasn't worth his time. I could feel this little hairline fracture in my left ventricle."

I opened my mouth to comfort him, but he shushed me.

"Wait! You'll miss the best part. So he gets this little sparkle in his eyes, and he smiles, right? And it's the cutest smile anyone has ever smiled. Have you ever noticed how soft his lips look? They *look* soft! How does that even happen?"

Opening the DVD case, I popped the movie into the machine and flashed Duckie a look to tell him to get on with the story already. "Stay on target. Are we ever getting to this miraculous kiss, or are we stuck on the texture of his skin?"

He ignored my remark. "Then he says, 'Speaking as Romeo, I can assure you that I like Mercutio better.'"

I sat beside him, nuzzling into the pillows. "What did you say?"

"I didn't say anything. My whole brain melted, and I forgot how to talk." He paused, as if he was out of breath again at the mere mention of it. "And then, he got closer, put his hands on my shoulders, and kissed me."

Grinning, I grabbed a handful of popcorn and asked, "What was it like?"

Duckie was staring at the television but not really watching it. He was somewhere else entirely. "It was like my heart imploded with glitter."

I smiled. The menu screen was up on the television, but neither one of us had pushed play. "Between your brain melting and that, I'd say he pretty much destroyed you with that kiss."

"Oh, in the best way possible." Finally managing to tear his gaze away from the screen, and himself from wherever it was that he'd gone in his head, he turned to face me. "It didn't last very long, but he was so gentle and sweet. Then afterward—because I still couldn't talk—"

"Because of your melted brain."

"Precisely." He nodded. "Afterward, he just kinda pulls back and smiles at me and says, 'I hope that was okay.' I told him, 'It was amazing.'"

"Ooh, good response. Who knew the cure for a melted brain was kissing?" I pressed play, but not to stop Duckie from talking. We had the movie memorized.

"I'm pretty sure that kissing might be the cure for everything." He sighed and lay back, looking up at all the cranes for a moment. "Anyway, he looked a little surprised, and then he said he thought it was beyond amazing. Shortly after that, I went and found you."

"That's fantastic." Grinning, I shoved another handful of popcorn into my mouth.

"It really was." He looked at me then, letting a little bit of Serious Duckie show through. "I like him, y'know? A lot. It'll be a shame when he finally breaks my heart."

I hated that he looked at things that way, that he couldn't just allow himself this one day to be happy and carefree. "Maybe he won't."

"Brooke, we're seniors in high school. Somebody is going to break somebody's heart in this scenario." The corner of his mouth lifted some in a forced half smile.

"That's optimistic," I said sarcastically. I reached into the bowl and grabbed more popcorn. This time, I fed it to Duckie.

As he chewed, he said, "I'm just a realist. But for the moment . . . I'm really, insanely happy."

"Be positive, Duckman. Who knows? Maybe you'll break his heart."

"One can only hope." On the screen, Andie had just run into her Duckie at school. We watched for a bit before my Duckie said, "So how are things between you and the cree—Derek? Did he apologize for sneaking in last night?"

"Things are good, and he did apologize. But I do wonder how he's feeling about me dumping him for you tonight."

"You'd dump anyone for me. And I'd dump anyone for you. That's just the way it is." It was true. Our friendship and theater: the only two things Duckie was absolutely confident about.

"I-L-Y, Duckie."

"I-L-Y."

We watched the movie for a while. Andie's dad was trying to talk her into going to prom. It felt weird that I wouldn't be Duckie's date this year. He'd be with Tucker, and I'd be with Derek. At least . . . I assumed I'd be with Derek. He hadn't asked me yet. Maybe I should have asked him. Maybe I would.

Because despite how I'd felt when I got out of Kingsdale, despite my irritation at Mom asking me about it, I really did want to go. It felt big, this moment of revelation. It felt . . . wonderful.

I could feel the cranes above us gesturing to my closet, but it took me a moment to realize what they were pointing at. When it hit me, my heart skipped a nervous beat. My razor was still in my closet. What if Duckie saw it? What if he thought I'd been faking my recent happiness and told my parents? I couldn't go back to Kingsdale. Especially not now.

My phone buzzed, making me jump. When I picked it up, Duckie said, "Hey. Rude. This is our night."

"It's Derek. I'll just text him back real quick and let him know I'm busy."

"Well, while you're doing that, I'm going to go grab another drink." Duckie opened my bedroom door and disappeared. The moment he was gone, I hurried to my closet and retrieved my razor. I tossed it in the small trash can by my desk, making certain to cover it up with some crumpled-up papers. I didn't need it anymore, and there was no sense in worrying anyone by keeping the stupid thing.

I settled back down among the pillows and looked at my

phone. Derek's message made me sit up a little.

He said, We need to talk, Brooke.

I typed in my response and hit send. I can't talk right now. Duckie's over. Can I call you after he leaves?

I was expecting a yes, but instead, he texted, I know what's going on.

I had no idea what he was talking about. Had he been drinking or something?

What are you talking about? What's going on?

A long pause. And then finally, his answer. I know what's going on between you and Duckie.

I have no idea what you're talking about. Are you okay? He had to be drunk. Or something. He was acting so weird.

I waited for a long time. Just when I thought he'd decided not to reply, another text popped up. Just tell me the truth. Are you and Duckie screwing around?

If I hadn't been so taken aback by the ridiculousness of his question, I might have laughed aloud. You do know he's gay, right? Of course we're not screwing around! Why would you even think that?

I waited to see the three dots that indicate the other person you're texting is writing something, but they didn't pop up. I texted, Duckie is just my friend. Besides, I'd never do that to you.

I waited again, but the dots still didn't show. I pulled up his number and put the phone to my ear. It rang again and again, until it finally went to voice mail. Something told me Derek was done talking with me for the night.

Duckie walked back into the room and immediately said, "What's wrong? You look like you might cry."

My bottom lip was trembling. "Derek has apparently gotten the idea in his head that you and I are screwing around."

"Together?" Duckie looked disgusted at the very idea. "Gross."

Tears were welling up in my eyes. Had I somehow misled Derek into thinking I was involved with Duckie in that way? Had I said something, done something to make him think so?

Duckie looked at me, misunderstanding the expression I wore. "Not gross gross. You know if I were into girls, I'd be hittin' that—"

"No. You wouldn't."

"—but the very idea of you and I . . . I mean, we're besties." He flopped down on the pillow pile beside me, looking just as shocked as I felt.

How could Derek think I'd hurt him like that? With anyone, let alone Duckie. It was crazy. "I have no idea why he'd think something like that. And now he won't return my texts or pick up when I call."

Duckie looked at me. "All this happened while I went to get a drink?"

Suddenly, all the confusion and pain burst out of me in the form of crying. Duckie sat down and put his arms around me, letting me soak his shirt in tears. "Hey. Don't worry about this. Derek just made a wrong assumption, that's all. You'll straighten it out."

My voice cracked. "How?"

He looked me in the eyes as he wiped away my tears with his hands. "First, you're going to munch on popcorn and finish watching this movie with me. Then you're going to get some sleep and go talk to him in person first thing in the morning. Just . . . go. Talk to him."

My lip was still shaking, and try as I might, I couldn't stop the tears from coming. What had I done wrong to make Derek act this way? "What if he won't listen?"

Duckie picked up the bowl of popcorn and set it in my lap. His words were definitive . . . and wise. But that didn't make them any easier to hear. "Then it's his loss."

CHAPTER FIFTEEN

The next morning, I got ready and did exactly as Duckie had suggested. I walked straight to Derek's house. He had to hear the honest truth about Duckie and me. He just had to listen. Because this was ridiculous. It was absurd. Had he been drinking? Or was it something else?

Maybe his depression was making him act out in anger. What if he'd hurt himself? I picked up the pace, hurrying my steps until I was running to his house. Oh god, what if he'd given in to his suicidal urges because he'd gotten it in his head that I didn't want to be with him?

By the time I reached his house, I was out of breath. His

dad's truck was in the driveway. For a moment, I debated going home and calling Derek instead. His dad didn't seem like the kind of person who wanted anyone knocking on his door. For any reason. Ever.

It felt like the longest walk in the world to go from the road to the front door, but when I reached it, catching my breath, I found my strength. If Derek was hurt—or worse—I'd call and get him help. If he wasn't hurt . . . if he'd just been acting possessive, I'd talk to him and try to figure out this misunderstanding. After I knocked, my heart started beating faster. When the door opened, it skipped a beat. Mostly in relief that Derek was still alive.

Derek looked like he hadn't slept. For some stupid reason, I felt immediately guilty for having slept just fine. I always slept well after a really hard cry. It was like my body would reboot itself to recover from the trauma.

The moment he saw me, his frown deepened. He didn't speak.

"Derek, can we talk?" My throat was still sore from crying last night. Even after the movie was over and Duckie had gone home, I'd sat up and cried, searching my memory for anything that I might have said or done to give Derek the wrong impression. I'd come up empty.

Derek grumbled, "Not here."

He stepped out, and the screen door closed behind him.

Just as we were stepping off the porch, a greasy man in a dirty tank top and jeans came to the door. There was an open beer in his hand and a slur in his speech. On his right hand was a ring—maybe a class ring from high school, I couldn't tell. It had to be his dad. "You get your ass back here in an hour or else, you little shit."

Derek didn't respond to him. He just picked up his pace.

His dad staggered out the door and pointed an accusing finger at me. "So you're the girlfriend who spends her nights with other guys. Boy, my son sure knows how to pick 'em. You're a real piece of work."

Derek gripped my arm as we walked, but I slowed my pace anyway as I looked at his dad. Relenting, Derek slowed too.

Slugging his beer down, the man swallowed and wiped his mouth with the back of his hand. His eyes burned into mine. "Don't get too comfortable with my son, girly. Don't think we'll be staying here too long."

I didn't know what to say to that, to him. After a moment, Derek's grip tightened on my bicep, and he tugged me down the driveway.

He didn't release his hold on my arm until we reached the road, and after that, we walked toward the park in silence. Derek's steps were hurried at first, and it took some effort for me to keep up. Once we were out of sight of his house, I said, "I don't know why you think something's going on between Duckie and me, but it's not. And I can't spend eternity repeating that to you. Do you believe me?"

He shoved his hands in the pockets of his hoodie and kept his eyes forward, his tone clipped. "You two do spend an awful lot of time together."

It was the first time that anyone had questioned my friendship with Duckie. "We've been best friends practically our whole lives."

His jaw tightened. He had yet to look at me since he'd answered the door. "You ditch me to spend time with him."

Remembering Duckie's words, I stopped in my tracks. He kept walking. "I'm not having this conversation. You either believe me or you don't."

His steps slowed, but he remained facing away from me for the longest time. When he finally turned to face me, his eyes were shimmering. "I don't want to break up."

"Neither do I. This is ridiculous. Look, I'm not going to spend less time with Duckie, but I want to spend more time with you."

He looked up into the overcast sky, swallowing the tears that threatened to fall. "I'm having a really hard time understanding what someone like you sees in someone like me."

I shook my head in wonder that someone as interesting,

intelligent, talented, and gorgeous could have such low self-esteem. "You happen to be a really fantastic person, Derek. But I think life has just beaten you down and made it so you can't see how great you really are."

He swallowed as he met my eyes. "Not just life."

I tilted my head in wonder. "What do you mean?"

"Last night after we texted, my dad came into my room and started screaming about how we never have any food in the house because I eat it all. Something about how he can't even have a damn sandwich when he wants one." Derek removed his hands from his pockets and raked his fingers through his hair. Stress radiated from him. "I was already upset about our conversation, so I mouthed off to him and told him exactly why we hardly ever have any food in the house. Because he's a shit father and a selfish alcoholic who spends all of his money on booze."

My heart sank into my stomach. He'd said his dad was an asshole. I only had a taste of how bad it really was at Derek's house and could already solidly agree with him on that.

"He grabbed my phone out of my hands and threw it against the wall. Totally smashed it. Then he gave me a little reminder to watch my mouth." Hesitantly, Derek lifted his hoodie and shirt up, revealing large bruises all over the left side of his body. One of the bruises looked like it might have been made by a man's ring.

My fingers shook as they found my mouth. "Derek. Oh my god. Are you okay? We need to get this looked at."

He pulled his clothes down over his wounds and shrugged, not meeting my eyes. "It hurts, but I've had worse. It'll heal."

Empathy for Derek and absolute anger at his father filled me. "You need to report him. Like now."

He threw me a look that said I had no idea what I was talking about. "To who?"

My mind raced. What kind of parent would treat his child that way? "The cops? Child Protective Services? Someone! I don't know."

"Brooke." He cupped my face gently in his hands. "I don't want anyone to know."

I placed my hands over his and met his gaze. "You have nothing to be ashamed of. The man is a monster. He should be locked up for how he treats you."

He touched his forehead to mine, and we both closed our eyes. His skin was warm, as was his breath on my neck. He spoke in pleading whispers. "I've never told anyone but you about him hitting me. I've never shown anyone my bruises before. Please promise me you won't tell anyone. Please, Brooke?"

An idea grabbed me and I straightened, dropping my hands to his shoulders. "When's your birthday?"

Derek furrowed his brow in question. "April eighth. Why?"

Perfect. "You'll be eighteen then. You could move out and get him out of your life."

He shook his head, and there was an annoyance in his eyes that I didn't understand. It had to be from what his dad had just put him through. "Where am I supposed to go exactly? Besides, you heard my dad. We'll probably be long gone before then. Once he gets it in his head to move, we move."

"Well, maybe you could stay. You could get a job and find a roommate for a few months. Or you might be able to stay with Duckie. And then this fall, you could move into the dorms." I took a step back, nodding at my brilliant idea. He'd be free then. He'd be safe.

"Dorms?"

"Yeah." I blinked at him, wondering why my words didn't seem to be reaching him. "College?"

Derek turned away from me for a moment. When he turned back, he was holding his hands out, palms up, and shaking his head. "I just asked you to keep this secret for me, and you're telling me to get a job and go to college?"

"I'm just trying to find a way out for you. For us. Maybe we could go to the same school." Images flooded my mind of Derek and me living on the same campus, going to college parties together, somewhere away from his father. Somewhere safe.

Derek's voice was flat. "I didn't think there were any colleges around here."

"There aren't. But there are some great schools in Michigan. We wouldn't even have to leave the state. Look at University of Michigan. Ann Arbor is awesome. Plus, it's not too late for you to apply. They consider late applicants on a case-by-case basis." The realization hit me that I actually was looking forward to hearing back from U of M. I *wanted* to be accepted. I *wanted* to go to college.

I *wanted* to live.

"Wait. After graduation, you're moving away?"

"Yeah. Maybe. I don't know." And I didn't know. But the fact that I could even see a future now that I was focusing more on what would come rather than how it would all end made me see that maybe the meds actually were working . . . and maybe all those Monopoly games with Dr. Daniels were helping too. I grabbed his hand in mine, squeezing it. "But the point is, you could come with me. We could be together. And you'd be safe."

He shook my hand away, rubbing his hands over his face and shaking his head. "You could have told me you were planning on leaving."

"It's been kind of a recent development." I furrowed my

brow, honestly confused by the way he was reacting to my solution. I was just trying to help him. "Don't you want to go to college?"

Derek shifted his weight from one leg to the other, his eyes on the direction of his house. "I just assumed I'd end up with a crappy job like my dad, living in a trailer in a shitty neighborhood or something. When you grow up like I have, Brooke, you don't think about college. You think about survival."

I stepped closer and gently took his hand back in mine. I was going too fast, and it was freaking him out. Tempering my enthusiasm for a moment, I said, "Well, maybe you could start thinking of college as a survival opportunity."

He was still peering down the road. I had no idea what he might be thinking. "Maybe. I don't know."

"Will you at least consider it?"

"Yes. But promise me you won't tell anyone about . . . my dad." When he looked at me, I could see the need in his eyes.

I placed a gentle kiss on his chin. "Of course I promise."

He slid his arms around me, pulling me into a hug. Last night's texts fell away into the midmorning haze. After a few seconds of silence, he cleared his throat. "Listen. I'm probably way wrong about you and your friend Duckie—"

"You are."

"—but I do feel like every time I spend time with you,

it's after I pull you away from something you're doing with him."

It was true. There was no denying that. I'd never been very good at balancing Duckie and a boyfriend—which was one of the reasons I'd had so few. But Derek was important to me. I wanted to make this work. "I'm sorry. I'm just used to having him around all the time. But you're right. I've been neglecting our time together. What can we do about that?"

He already looked somewhat relieved. "Hmm. It's Friday. I heard there's a party tonight. If you're interested."

"I'm totally interested. I just have to tell my parents the makeup crew is having a working party tonight. Kind of a celebration of all our hard work so far mingled with time to sort out some costuming issues? Duckie will back me up." My eyes fell to his torso and I thought about the bruises just under two layers of relatively thin fabric. "You sure you're feeling up to it?"

"Believe me. Anything that will get me out of the house . . . Besides, it's you. And I need to be with you." He bent down and brushed my lips in a tender kiss. All, apparently, had been forgiven.

Maybe I was reading too much into it, but it seemed like Derek had been a bit clingy since we'd first had sex. But he was my boyfriend. He was supposed to want more of my time and attention. Wasn't he?

I hesitated before saying what else I was thinking, but finally managed to blurt it out. "What if I ask Duckie and Tucker to come along? That way, maybe you'll see that there's only friendship between Duckie and me."

Derek managed a smile. "Okay. The party's at some farm on Wilson Road."

"I know the place. Duckie will have to drive us. It's kinda in the middle of nowhere. What time should we leave?"

"From what I hear, things should start to get really interesting around eleven."

"Then we'll pick you up a few minutes before that." I hugged him gently, not wanting to aggravate his injuries. When I met his eyes, I said, "I'm glad we talked."

"Me too." He kissed me on the tip of my nose, his smile broadening with relief. "See you tonight."

As we began to part, I tilted my head at him with a question. "You sure you're okay to go home?"

"I have to go home eventually. I'll be okay. I promise." His words said that he'd be just fine. His tone said that he was scared to go home. He turned and started walking back to his house. As he did, he said, "Eleven."

"Eleven," I said, watching my boyfriend move down the road alone toward his house. The thought of how good sex with Derek was filled my head. It was intense. Amazing. I'd felt whole, like two pieces of a complicated puzzle had at last come together (no pun intended). But this moment felt exactly the opposite of that. This was intense too, but in direct contrast to that. There had to be a way to restore the good feelings of that night at his house and erase the off-kilter feeling of this moment. It made total sense that Derek was feeling needy and even betrayed, growing up with a dad like he had. I just had to show him that not everyone intended to inflict pain on someone—that I'd really meant it every time I'd professed my love to him.

Maybe he'd understand that after the party. I hoped to hell he would.

We pulled up in front of Derek's place at eleven o'clock and waited. I didn't dare knock on the door to let him know we were there. The last thing I wanted was a repeat of that morning's encounter—especially now that I'd seen how abusive his dad could really get. The very idea that someone couldn't contain their anger and would violently lash out at another person—their own kid, even—really frightened me. I was scared for Derek. I hoped he was taking my college suggestion seriously.

Derek came out the front door and made his way into the backseat with me. It was so weird to sit in the Beast with anyone but Duckie, or to sit anywhere but my spot on the passenger's side. But now Tucker was there, and Derek and I were in the back together. I sat on the foam side, just to be nice, but I didn't think he really noticed. It made me think about how long Duckie and I had been sharing rides in the Beast, but this time in a way that made me feel a little more than sad. What would happen when the day came that Duckie and I had college classes, jobs, obligations, and relationships? The day would have to come that the Beast would stop running, and both of us would have lives that didn't consist of classes and hanging out. Wouldn't it? Or could friendships last forever?

Derek pulled the door shut behind him and said, "Hey."

From the driver's seat, Duckie put on his best-behavior tone and said, "Hey, Derek."

On our way to pick up Tucker, I'd told Duckie about my talk with Derek—leaving out the subject of his dad's abuse, as promised—and about how Derek was seriously concerned that Duckie and I might have a thing going on. It really was a ridiculous notion to think of Duckie and me hooking up, but I was hoping that maybe hanging out tonight might show Derek how unrealistic his concerns really were.

The Beast smelled like cotton linen, which meant that Duckie had purchased some new air freshener—probably because he didn't want Tucker to associate his first night out with Duckie with the smell of Fritos. As we tore down the road, Derek reached over and took my hand in his. The boys chatted as Duckie drove us deep into nowhere, and I looked out the window at the blanket of stars above us. Duckie was being on his absolute best behavior, but I couldn't tell if that was because he was trying to impress Tucker or if he was trying to assure Derek that he was totally harmless.

After a while, Duckie turned onto a dirt driveway and parked the Beast alongside about a dozen other cars—every one of them in better condition than the Beast, but not one of them nearly as cool. Music was pouring out of the farmhouse already, and colored lights filled the windows. The Kerrington farm had been abandoned for something like ten years, but kids had been holding parties here for the past six or seven. The cops knew about it but pretty much ignored the law breaking, so long as it didn't get out of hand and nobody got hurt. I'd only been to two parties at the farm before this one, but Duckie had been to those two and then some.

Duckie's parents were far more lenient than mine. Prior to my stay in Kingsdale, mine had always been pretty cool about my social life, so long as they had a vague idea of where I was, who I was with, and what I was doing. Naturally, I told them as little as possible, and nothing about parties at the Kerrington farm. It was nice that they were backing off now a bit. Still, it would be nice if I didn't have to lie about going to a party.

We all got out of the Beast and walked toward the house, Derek holding my hand. Duckie and Tucker walked closely together but didn't touch. Something told me that would change by the end of the evening.

People were pouring into the house. It looked like the party of the year. As we stepped through the front door, all the sounds and sights hit us at once. The buzz of the large generator sitting to the right of the door. A band playing at the back of the house, the bass thumping deeply in my chest. Somebody had rigged up DJ lights, filling the entire house with colors and what looked like tiny, blinking groups of stars. The house was full of people laughing and talking while clutching red plastic cups filled with beer. Sarah Emberson and Kristah Neil were cackling up a storm as we passed—not at me, but their laughter did send a cold sharpness up my spine. Jake Taylor was looking them both over like maybe he'd had just enough booze to get the courage to hit on one of them—either of them. Jake wasn't exactly a picky guy.

We navigated our way through the crowd with some effort. Duckie and Tucker were soon swallowed by the darkness, disappearing to who knew where in the enormous old house. Derek gave my hand a squeeze. I looked at him and he said something, but I couldn't hear him over the noise. Apparently he took that as a yes to whatever he was asking me, because he led me through the house until we stepped into what had been the kitchen. In the center of the room was a keg. Derek grabbed two cups and filled them rather expertly before handing me one. I didn't bother telling him that I didn't drink beer. Instead I shouted, "Thank you," and hoped he heard over the noise.

He stepped closer and put his mouth right by my ear. "Quite a party."

I spoke into his ear so that he could hear. "It's loud. We should go upstairs."

He nodded, and I grabbed his hand and led him back through the room where the band was playing and up the stairs. There were fewer people up here, and the music was plenty loud but more bearable. At the top of the stairs was a big loft, and standing to the right were Duckie and Tucker, who'd apparently had the same idea that we'd had about the noise. They were both grinning and chatting. Neither of them had a beer or any other kind of drink. Apparently, each other's company was enough to make their heads swim. My heart overflowed with promise for my best friend.

We joined the two of them, and Duckie glanced at the cup in my hand and raised his eyebrows before shaking his head. Maybe he thought Derek was a bad influence on me. It wasn't like I was drinking the beer. It was more like I was serving as a cup holder. Derek took a healthy gulp from his cup. After he swallowed, he smiled at me. "I'm glad I came."

I smiled back. "Me too."

We hung out in the loft, people watching and telling dirty jokes, until Derek convinced Tucker to chug the beer I was holding. As Tucker started downing it, Duckie looked less than pleased. Seeing the intensity of his glare, I began to wonder if the Duckman would be able to hold his tongue all night. But an hour later, Duckie had his left arm around Derek's shoulder and his right arm around Tucker. They were singing songs from *Phantom of the Opera* as loudly and as obnoxiously as they could and laughing their faces off. Tucker had two more beers as the night progressed. Derek had three. Duckie taught us all how to moonwalk.

To my great surprise, Claire Simpson was in the corner making out hardcore with Scott Melbur. We're talking hands up her top, her mouth devouring his entire face making out. It was almost comical. I could just imagine the title in the school paper now: "Cheer Captain Gives Yearbook Photographer Something to Cheer About!"

Party of the year, indeed.

"Brooke! Brooke Danvers!" I turned to see who was calling my name and my eyes fell on Michael Stein. I waved him over, and as soon as he reached me, he said, "Have you seen Claire anywhere?"

I decided to spare him some heartbreak and not mention that I had seen Claire . . . and her lips on some other guy.

"Afraid not. So what are you doing here, anyway? You don't usually hit these parties."

Sadness lurked in his eyes. "I just . . . my sister, Samantha?"

I knew Samantha. She was only five years old, and she'd been diagnosed with something called Tay-Sachs disease when she was just a baby. And she was the center of Michael's world. In fact, when Michael's parents had suggested he get involved in school plays, he'd initially refused, not wanting to leave his sister's side. He said he'd feel selfish doing them. But eventually, he came around, and the plays were a welcome distraction from the stress and sadness that awaited him at home. From what Michael had told me, there was no cure for the disease.

"It's just . . . She's taken a turn for the worse. I wanted to see Claire tonight, because I don't think I'll be at school much soon. Very soon, if the doctors are right. And I don't want anything to go unsaid." He met my eyes, hoping I got what he was trying to convey to me. "Y'know?"

I knew. I understood every word that Michael was saying, along with every word that he wasn't saying. Samantha was dying. And he needed a moment to really live his life before his baby sister's death wrapped him up in a cocoon of misery and mourning.

I fought back tears. Tears for Samantha. Tears for their family. Tears for Michael and all the pain that he must have been experiencing. Then I hugged him and said, "I'm here for you. Just know that, okay? If you ever need to talk, you can call me anytime you need."

"Thanks, Brooke. You're a good friend."

As we parted, I saw Derek approaching. Drying my eyes, I said to Michael, "Hey, I want you to meet my boyfriend, Derek."

The next few seconds were a blur. Derek had stepped hard toward Michael, and then his arm was flying through the air. Time broke down into flashes of movement. Derek's fist connecting with Michael's face. Michael's head thrown back from the blow. Blood spattering from his nose.

Once time began running normally again, I realized that Tucker had pulled Derek off Michael, who was leaning on the railing of the loft, his head bent down, blood dripping onto the floor. As Tucker pulled Derek away, Derek wrenched back toward Michael, pointing at him and growling, "You touch her again, I'll knock your damn teeth outta your head."

My feet were frozen to the floor. I was aware of the colors

and sounds, but it felt as if my world had shattered. Duckie tried to put his arms around me, but I pushed him away and made my way down the stairs, after Tucker and Derek. When I got outside, Duckie not long after me, Tucker was standing near the door. Derek was pacing back and forth outside, cursing under his breath.

When I tried to approach him, Tucker reached out to stop me, but Duckie shook his head. I shoved at Derek's right shoulder. "Derek, what the hell was that?"

His chest rose and fell quickly, and he shouted at me. I wondered if his dad sounded like this when he got mad. "Jesus, Brooke. That guy was trying to screw you! How can you not see that?"

I'd never had anyone shout at me like that. Not with fury in their eyes and blood on their mind. It scared me. But more than anything, it gave me a bit of clarity. "That's it. I'm done. Duckie, take me home."

Derek stopped pacing at last, as if he could talk some sense into me. But I wasn't the one missing any sense at the moment. He said, "Brooke..."

"No. I am done, Derek. We are over." I walked over to the Beast. Derek came after me, but Tucker blocked his path. I don't know what Tucker said to him, but Derek eventually nodded and went back inside the house. Tucker and Duckie joined me by the car. Once the doors were unlocked, we all climbed inside in absolute, horrified silence.

No one said a word the entire ride back to my house.

Mostly because there was nothing to be said.

CHAPTER SIXTEEN

It had been days since I'd told Derek that it was over, and just when I thought I was out of tears, that my emotional well had run dry, I started crying again. There was a pile of tissues surrounding the trash can in Dr. Daniels's office, and several more tissues inside of it. Which meant both that I was a seriously crappy shot and that I'd broken my rule of not crying inside a therapist's office. The doc handed me a new tissue and said, "Does Derek have a history of violence?"

"No." I didn't bring up Derek's dad's abuse. That was his dad's history of violence, not his.

"What about jealousy?"

I blew my nose and threw another tissue into the trash can. Swish. "He thought Duckie and I were hooking up. But I told him we weren't."

The doc was sitting across from me, his tone caring and concerned. "He didn't believe you?"

"No. That's actually why we went to the party. So I could show him that I had nothing to hide from him. And then he just lost it." Tears streaked my cheeks. All I could see when I closed my eyes were the droplets of blood that had flown through the air after Derek's fist had connected. "I shouldn't have hugged Michael."

"Why do you say that?"

The nightmare of the droplets of blood gave way to the image of Michael hanging his head as more blood poured from his face to the floor. And for what? For my shitty timing, that's what. "Because it was loud in there, and Derek couldn't hear our interaction to tell we were just friends. And I didn't explain who Michael was before I stepped away from Derek and hugged him. No wonder Derek thought I was fooling around."

"That's not fair to you, Brooke." He leaned forward, resting his elbows on his thighs, folding his fingers together. "Just because you're in a relationship doesn't mean that anyone has the right to lay their hands on anyone else because they have a jealous streak. Derek was in the wrong here."

"Then why do I feel so guilty?" Another bout of sobbing came on and I cried hard for a full minute before the doc handed me some more tissues and I could calm down enough to continue our discussion.

"Maybe because you're searching for a reason to forgive him so that you can be with him again." He glanced out the window, and when he looked back at me, I could see that this wasn't just advice from the therapist in him. The doc could relate on a personal level. Seemingly without being aware of it, he fiddled with the gold band that was on his left ring finger once again and said, "Stranger things have happened."

I dried my eyes, still sniffling. "What happened to you, anyway?"

Realizing that I was gesturing to his wedding ring with my eyes, he sat up straight in his chair. "That's not an appropriate subject between a therapist and a patient."

"Come on, doc. I'll show you my wounds if you show me yours."

He paused. Noticeably. "It doesn't work that way."

It was my turn to lean forward, closing the space between us. "Please. I want to know."

The doc sat there for a good, long time, eyeing the ring on his finger and obviously debating how much was ethical to share with me. Finally, he said, "My wife of ten years had an affair with her boss. It lasted three years before I caught them. She moved out six months ago, and I still find myself lying awake at night, wondering what I did to drive her away." He looked into my eyes. "But it wasn't my fault that she made poor decisions, Brooke. Just like it isn't your fault that Derek lost his temper in a fit of jealousy and punched an innocent guy."

The doc was all right. Human, even. "I wish I didn't miss him so much. I wish I hated him. It would be easier. Y'know?"

"Yes, I do."

The Monopoly board on the table between us was spattered with wet spots from all my tears. "I'm sorry I cried all over the bank."

"That's okay. It'll dry out. No big deal." The doc smiled at me. Maybe he felt better about his own situation now that he'd said something. I know I felt a bit better about mine. We'd both begun picking up the game and putting the pieces of it back into the box when the doc said, "Listen. I think it would be best if you take some time to focus on yourself and your mental health. Give this thing with Derek some distance. Can you do that?"

"I can try."

"Good." Pausing with a stack of Community Chest cards in his hand, he looked at me. "Do you think that Derek would ever try to physically hurt you?"

"No." Of course he wouldn't. Derek loved me. I was sure of it.

"Okay then." Once the game was put away, we both stood, and he offered me a raised eyebrow. "Next week? Same bat time, same bat channel?"

"As long as I get to be the top-hat-wearing thimble, then yeah." A chuckle escaped me, surprising me. It felt wrong somehow to laugh at all when you were in pain. There was a strange sense of guilt that came with it.

As I walked out of Dr. Daniels's office, my phone buzzed with a text. When I looked at the screen, my heart ached. It was from Derek. Apparently he'd gotten a new phone.

I miss you.

Holding the phone in my hand, I stared at the words and thought about the space that the doc had urged me to take. Derek texted again.

I'm sorry.

I slid my phone into my pocket without answering.

The doc was right. I needed my space.

CHAPTER SEVENTEEN

Change was difficult, but I took the doc's advice and made some time to focus on myself and put all the stuff with Derek in a box at the back of my mind. Luckily, the play was an incredible distraction. Michael was looking over a table full of various creams and powders. His face was still bruised and swollen, and every time I looked at him, I wanted to cry and apologize for Derek's outburst. But I got the distinct impression that Michael didn't want that. He wasn't mad at me. He was just hurt and probably pretty scared that Derek might do something like that again.

He pointed to one jar and said, "What about this shade

of pancake for Romeo's face?"

I picked up the one next to it. "Tucker has pretty tan skin. I think this might work better. Don't you think?"

He nodded. "You're right. Now if we can just get his lips covered . . . or is that the Duckman's department?"

We shared a chuckle, and after, I said, "Listen. Michael, I'm sorry about Derek."

"Brooke. Don't. Okay? It's not your fault." His eyes held the deepest sincerity. "But I'd think twice about hanging around a guy like that. What if he'd hurt you instead of me?"

"I can handle Derek."

"I couldn't."

Things got quiet between us for a while. Eventually, I went over and helped out the set builders before running lines with a few of the actors. That was something about theater—even if you didn't get along or hang out on the outside of it, when you were one of us, you were one of our own. It was a real sense of family.

At least I wasn't invisible at rehearsal. I was tangible. It felt nice.

I also wasn't feeling such despair. Despite my problems with Derek, I was feeling pretty light on my feet. Suddenly hope seemed like something more than just bullshit. It seemed real. And I had it.

Duckie ran up to me, a look of utter joy plastered on his

face. "Did you see the costume I'm going to be wearing?"

"I just did! It's hot, Duckie."

"That's what Tucker said." If it had been possible for cartoon hearts to float out of his ears, they would have. It was adorably annoying.

"We should go to a Renaissance festival in costume sometime." Right after I said it, Duckie's face brightened even more. I blinked at him. "What? It's not exactly a big stretch for us to go from stage to jousting tournaments."

"It's just nice to hear you making plans for the future, that's all."

A smile settled on my lips. It *felt* nice too. "Oh, hey, I forgot my backpack in my locker earlier. Can you distract the powers that be while I grab it?"

"No problem."

Duckie was the best.

I navigated my way through the halls to my locker. When I reached it, my heart sank into my stomach. Sticking out of it was a small, black envelope. The note inside wasn't signed, but I knew it was from Derek. In silver text, it read simply, "I love you."

Missing Derek was hard. Loving him had been so easy. How had we come to this?

When I got back to the gym, I was going to tell Duckie, but he and Tucker were standing so close. The rest of the world didn't exist for them in that moment. Just each other. They looked so happy, and I wasn't about to intrude on that.

As I walked past them to the makeup station, Duckie said, "Hey, are you okay?"

I gave him a false smile and shrugged but kept walking. "Yeah, fine."

The rest of practice flew by in a haze.

By the time we got home that night, my mom and dad had already loaded their bags into the car. It had taken Dad a lot of convincing Mom that I'd be fine with only Duckie there to keep me company, but he'd triumphed, to my great relief. I was barely out of the Beast when Mom hugged me super tight. "Oh, sweetie, are you sure you'll be all right?"

Behind her, Dad rolled his eyes in a playful way.

"I'll be fine. Besides, it's not like I'll be alone."

Duckie shut the driver's door of the Beast and beamed. Mom wrung her hands a bit, but finally Dad said, "Come on, Joanne. We're going to be late. We have our phones if they need anything."

"Okay." She said it, but I wasn't sure if she was speaking to herself or us. "Okay, this'll be fine."

Dad opened her door and practically had to shove her into the car. As he walked around to get into the driver's seat, she looked out the open window at me. "All the contact and emergency numbers are on the fridge. Call if you need anything. Even if you just feel like talking, okay?"

"Have fun!" Duckie waved, and Dad pulled the car out of the driveway. Once they were out of sight, the Duckman and I exchanged eye rolls. He said, "Dude. That was annoyingly painful. Movie time?"

"Movie time."

Twenty minutes later, once we'd settled in my room with a pile of DVDs to pick from, he flopped on my bed and said, "So why'd you lie to me earlier?"

"What are you talking about?"

"You were fine. Well, fine-ish. And then you weren't. Why?"

Reaching into my backpack, I retrieved Derek's note and handed it to Duckie. "I found this in my locker."

After Duckie read it, he returned it to me. There was something in his eyes that I hadn't often seen in the years since we'd been friends. Absolute anger. "Do you want me to tell him to knock it off?"

"No. I just miss him." I returned the note to my backpack and dropped it on the floor next to my desk. "I mean, I know he has a temper. But I miss him."

Duckie appeared to be doing all he could to remain calm and not shake me senseless. "You miss him, and that's totally okay. But Brooke, the guy attacked Michael for no reason. Not to mention getting kicked out of school for roughing up

Eric Squires over writing on your locker."

"He thought he was protecting me." I could hear the excuses, my defense of Derek, leaving my mouth. But even I didn't believe them anymore. How could I love someone who was capable of such things? What did that say about me?

Duckie was finished treating me with kid gloves. "So what happens the day you seriously piss him off? Is he going to hit you too?"

Confidently, I said, "He wouldn't do that. Derek would never hurt me."

"You sure? Because I'm not." I knew his words came from a place of concern, but I didn't want to hear them.

"Let's just watch the movie," I said, putting in the *High Fidelity* DVD. We almost made it all the way through too, but at some point, our busy day of rehearsal and the long week caught up to us, and we dozed off before the credits rolled. I wasn't sure how much time had passed before Duckie stirred and moved out of the room. He probably had to pee or something. As my eyes began to flutter closed once again, I noticed something on the window. It looked like words.

Slowly, I approached the dew-covered glass. Written in the moisture were the words "I need you. Forgive me."

My heart was thumping loudly in my ears. Had Derek been watching me? Watching us? On the other side of the glass on the windowsill lay a red rose. I glanced over my shoulder, wondering when Duckie would return. Soon, I imagined. I reached up and unlocked the window. Slowly, I pulled it open and stretched my hand out, picking up the rose.

A hand closed over my wrist, and I jumped with a yelp.

"Shh. It's just me." Derek smiled at me. "Sorry. Didn't mean to scare you. I was hoping we could talk."

I stepped back from the window. As Derek crawled into my room, I said, "Derek! You shouldn't be here. You should go."

Duckie had left the room only a moment ago. What would he say when he came back to find Derek in my room? Would he tell my parents?

Derek held his hands palms up, his wide eyes full of pain and looking underslept. "I miss you. I'm sorry. I've screwed things up so badly between us, and I want to make it right. Please. Give me a chance to prove my love to you."

The doc's advice echoed in the back of my mind. "I think I need some time. Some space to think things over."

"What's to think about?" He took a step toward me, and when I took a step back, he looked hurt and confused. "Don't you love me anymore?"

"Of course I do." And I did. I'd never lie to him about something so important. "I'm just feeling a little . . . I don't know."

"I never meant to hurt you. Just like I'm sure you never meant to hurt me. I just . . . I need you in my life, Brooke. I can't stand the idea of losing you. You're my . . . my everything." He moved closer, slowly, and I fought to remain where I was standing.

As he brushed my hair away from my neck and placed a kiss on my collarbone, I said, "Derek, you need to go."

He stood straight, his shoulders looming over me, his eyes darkening. "I'm not going anywhere. Not until you talk to me."

"Get out. Please."

Derek shook his head. When he spoke again, his voice boomed throughout my bedroom. I shuddered at the sound of it. "That's not you talking. That's everybody standing in our way, trying to keep us apart. Stop letting them do this to us!"

Duckie ran breathlessly into the room, his cell phone in hand. "Derek! Get the hell out of here before I call the cops. I mean it."

At first, Derek didn't move. Then he slowly made his way to the window and climbed onto the roof. Once he was out, he turned back and growled at me, his eyes fierce and frightening. "You have to forgive me eventually."

After hurrying to close and lock the window, I turned back to Duckie, my heart racing. He said, "I should call the cops."

"Duckie, no." Derek had scared me, but I didn't want him to go to jail. I could only imagine what his dad might do to him after that.

"Then we have to call your parents."

I hesitated before speaking, and Duckie noticed. "That's probably a good idea."

He sighed and dropped his arm to his side, phone still in hand. "So why don't you seem keen on it? What part of what just transpired says not to call . . . I dunno . . . someone?"

If I was honest, it was the part of me that still cared about Derek, the part of me that didn't want to see him hurt. But I couldn't say that. Not even to Duckie.

"Brooke." His tone was sharp. "I've been covering for you, lying for you ever since Derek stepped into the picture. I'm not doing that anymore. I think we're well past the point of keeping a boyfriend secret from your parents now, don't you? This has crossed over into serious stalker territory. If you don't tell your parents what just happened, then I will."

I reached for his phone, but he moved his arm and I missed. "You wouldn't! Duckie, please. I just . . . everything will be fine, okay? And if he acts like that again, I'll tell my parents everything. Just not yet, okay?"

There was a fire in his eyes—one I'd never seen before. "Give me one good reason."

All that was left was the truth. Tears welled in my eyes as

I spoke the words, but I wasn't completely certain whether they were out of concern for Derek or fear for myself. "Derek's dad beats the shit out of him for no reason. I can't even imagine what he'd do if the cops showed up on his doorstep or if my dad gave him a call. So just . . . please. Don't."

A long, tense silence filled the room. Finally, with a sigh, Duckie plugged his phone into the charger on my desk and lay down on the makeshift bed on the floor. I crawled into bed with nothing more to say and no idea what to do.

Reaching up, I switched the light off, bathing us in darkness. After a moment, Duckie had the final word.

"I won't lie for you again."

My heart ached. I couldn't be sure about Duckie, but I didn't sleep for the rest of the night.

CHAPTER EIGHTEEN

For days, I struggled to find the right way to tell my parents about what had been going on. About the fact that I'd been sneaking around with a guy and asking Duckie to cover for me . . . to lie for me. They were going to be mad. At me. At Duckie. But more than that—the part that made it most excruciating to tell them about it—they were going to be hurt that I hadn't told them in the first place.

When I saw Derek at school on Monday, he was acting totally normal. A bit on the distant side, but normal. And when Duckie asked if I'd come clean to my parents, I told him I was trying to figure out the best time and way to explain the situation to them and that I was trying to find the right way to get Derek help. Duckie said the best way to do both of those things was just to come clean with my parents . . . but I wasn't convinced that would help Derek at all. I promised I'd tell them by the next weekend, and, thankfully, Duckie believed me. After that, the week was pretty much back to business as usual.

Stretching my right arm upward, I poked the thumbtack into the ceiling over my bed, hanging the crane I'd just folded with the others. My entire bedroom ceiling was covered with them. But that one was special. That one was just for me.

Duckie was lying on my bed, his head on my pillow, looking up at the cranes with an expression I could only describe as wonderment. "Did you know you've folded a thousand paper cranes? I've been counting how many are up there as you've been hanging them."

Looking at my ceiling, I wondered how the count had gotten so high. "That's a lot. I had no clue."

I batted gently at the one I'd just hung. The action reverberated through the entire collection. They were flying. Flying and free.

Duckie sat up, smiling at me. "Y'know, I heard that in Japan, a thousand origami cranes is supposed to grant you a wish. So . . . what are you going to wish for?"

The cranes flitted back and forth across my ceiling, and I wondered when the time would come to take them down. Eventually, I imagined. "I have no idea."

"There has to be something you want."

Biting my bottom lip for a moment, I thought back to Joy, the girl who'd taken her life while I was inpatient. I scanned the thousand cranes until I found the one with the bloody wing. Surrounding it, as if they were guarding it, were the several cranes I'd folded in the weeks after I'd returned home. "Right now, I just want to take these cranes down."

At first, he didn't say anything. Then he said, "You do?"

"Yeah. I do." I smiled down at Duckie, whose eyes were tearing up. It felt good, being in this place in my life. It was hard to imagine that I'd been in Kingsdale not that long ago. "And I think we should take them down to Black River to let them go. Kinda say good-bye to the past. Y'know?"

"I think that's an excellent idea." Duckie stood up beside me, admiring my work. "But how are we gonna carry a thousand origami cranes?"

"We'll stuff as many as we can inside my backpack. Even if we don't get them all, it's the symbolism that counts."

Duckie retrieved my backpack from beside my desk, and, ever so carefully, I began removing cranes from the ceiling—beginning with Joy's. Soon my backpack was stuffed. My ceiling was still mostly covered. As we headed downstairs for the front door, my dad said, "Hey, you two. Where are you off to?"

He and Mom were sitting in the living room. The news reporter on the TV was talking about a fire in the cemetery in the next town over. I swallowed hard before speaking. "We're going to Black River."

Mom sat up straight. She and Dad exchanged looks of concern.

"It's okay, you guys. Really. I just think it's time I put some stuff behind me."

After a long pause, Dad said, "Be home in time for dinner."

Mom looked like she didn't know exactly what to say, so she said, "I'm making lemon chicken."

They were worried. And I supposed they had every right, every reason. I'd put them through hell. "I'll be back in an hour or so. I promise."

We stepped outside, and Duckie grabbed my hand and started running for no apparent reason. After a moment, he let go, and we raced down the road, all the way to the park entrance. Duckie won. But only because he cheated by failing to announce that we were racing. Once we reached the bridge, Duckie said, "You never talk about that night."

One moment, I was standing on the bridge in broad

daylight. The next, I was standing there alone, at night, ready to end my life. I took a deep breath in and let it out slowly. The daylight returned—I was once more in the here and now. The other scene seemed like a bad dream to me. "You're right. I don't."

"Why not?"

"Because it's embarrassing and awful to think about." I slipped my backpack from my shoulders and unzipped it. The cranes inside sat up anxiously. They were ready to go, and I was ready to have them gone. I lifted them out in handfuls and tossed them into the water below. Each bunch flowed with the water, and soon my backpack was empty and the river contained a long line of origami cranes. They moved south, waving their tiny wings in a gesture of farewell. All but Joy's crane. Hers was leading the way, I was certain.

We watched them float away, and finally, Duckie reached over and took my hand in his. "Be honest. Do you ever still think about committing suicide?"

"Sometimes, but only in flitting thoughts in really dark moments. And those are a rarity lately. You have nothing to worry about." Before my attempt, I worried about Duckie a lot. What would he be like without a built-in audience and someone who really understood him? What would a sensitive guy like him do after losing his best friend? It was hard to think about.

"I don't want you thinking that way. Not ever. You're here. And I'm here. We're sticking together, and you're staying alive." I swore I heard a crack in his voice. He turned back to the river and watched the cranes shrink in the distance. Then, very quietly, he said, "Because you're my best friend and I love you too much to ever lose you."

My chest fluttered. Duckie and I never said the words. We'd only ever said I-L-Y.

He gave my hand a squeeze, and I squeezed back. He stood wordlessly beside me for a long time. Choking up, I said, "I love you too, Duckie."

His eyes were shimmering when he glanced at me. We gave the cranes a final wave and left the river—and all that it stood for—behind. As we headed home, Duckie changed the subject to more comfortable territory. Who would win in a slap fight: Brendon Urie from Panic! At the Disco or Pete Wentz from Fall Out Boy? Duckie pointed out that Pete might put up a good fight, but Brendon would probably fight dirty and beat him to death with a guitar. Any guitar.

It was hard to argue with that kind of logic.

Once we reached my house, I told Duckie that I needed to be alone. At first, he looked really concerned. But then a lightbulb went on over his head, and he understood. I was ready to tell my parents everything. Well . . . almost everything. They didn't need to know about me having sex or riding a motorcycle. Baby steps.

After the Beast rumbled its way down the road, I went inside and found my parents where I'd left them. My chest tight, I said, "Hey, guys. I need to talk to you." I spilled my guts for about a half hour, explaining that I'd been seeing Derek for several weeks. I told them about sneaking out, about lying and making Duckie lie for me. And then I told them about the night that Derek had come into my room without an invite and snuggled with me. I thought my dad was going to have a heart attack. The vein in his forehead popped out as I was talking. But he didn't say anything. Neither did Mom. They just sat there and listened as quietly and as calmly as they could. When I eventually got to the night Duckie had almost called the police, my voice shook. "I know we should have called . . . someone. But I was worried—I'm still worried—about what will happen to Derek. His dad might hurt him . . . or he might hurt himself. So, I'm sorry. For all of it. But I couldn't go on lying to you both. You deserve better than that."

There was a long, drawn-out silence. Then my parents both stood up. I was bracing for a lot of yelling and a severe punishment. Instead, they both hugged me tight. Tears coated my mom's cheeks as she said, "We love you so much, Brooke. Thank you for telling us about all of that."

My dad kissed the top of my head. "We're just glad you're

okay. And we'll figure out a way to help that boy, don't you worry about that."

For the rest of the day, we hung out in the living room together. Dad started to pull out the Monopoly board, but I opted for a game of Parcheesi instead. Afterward, we ate dinner and then watched *The Breakfast Club*. My parents, it turned out, weren't there to judge me. They just wanted to help me.

Just as Molly Ringwald was teaching the others how to put on lipstick with your cleavage, my phone buzzed, and I somehow knew who it was. With a deep breath, I looked at Derek's text.

I just keep doing stupid shit, don't I? I'm sorry, Brooke. I understand you need your space. I'll back off, if you want.

After some consideration, I texted back. I'm sorry things are like this between us.

Maybe they won't always be. We'll take some time off and then we can talk whenever you want to. He paused and then added, If you want to.

I had to admit, I was a bit taken aback by his sensitivity and respect after the way he'd spoken to me over a week ago. The least I could do was to show him the same respect. Thank you, Derek.

There was a long stretch of time before I saw those telling

three dots on my phone's screen. Could I see you one last time, just to apologize in person for the way I've been acting? I totally get it if you don't want to.

I swallowed the lump in my throat and glanced back at Dad, who was dozing in his chair. Mom had already fallen asleep on the couch. Everything in my gut said to stay here, to not see Derek. But another part of me knew that depending on what my parents decided to do, this might be the last chance I had to see Derek before everything changed. I moved my thumbs over the keys quickly and hit send before I could change my mind. Okay. But just for a few minutes. Meet me at the corner by my house in a half hour?

I felt bad for sneaking out again, but it would only be for a few minutes, and I owed Derek some closure. He'd had enough pain and betrayal in his life. I didn't want to add to it any more than I had to. Dad started snoring, so I crept to the front door, leaving my sleeping parents behind.

When I reached the corner, he was standing there, holding an open soda and looking sadder than I'd ever seen him. "Hey."

"Hey." He looked me up and down, as if memorizing me. After a moment of awkward silence, he said, "You want the rest of this? I'm just not as thirsty as I thought I was."

I took the soda from him and said, "Thanks. I'm . . . I'm sorry. For all of this."

"You have nothing to be sorry for. I was the one who messed things up between us."

As I thought of a response, I hid behind drinks of Derek's soda. What did you say to someone whose heart you'd broken into a million pieces? Especially when you still loved them.

I took another drink and said, "No one person is responsible for a relationship breaking up. It's my fault too."

He nodded, quiet and subdued. "So, we're really broken up, then?"

My head filled with the strangest fog. One minute I was holding the soda can in my hand, the next it was falling to the ground. Everything started to move in slow motion. I stepped toward Derek, but fell. "Something's . . . something's wrong."

The last thing I remembered was Derek catching me in his arms and telling me that everything was going to be just fine. Perfect, even.

But as I was swallowed by darkness, my gut said that something was very, very wrong.

CHAPTER NINETEEN

When I came to, it didn't feel like waking up from a night's sleep. It felt like what I imagined a hangover might feel like, or how my meds had made me feel until a few weeks ago, times ten. My head hurt like crazy, and I still felt like I was lost in a weird, hazy, sleepy fog. It felt like a dream, but I didn't pinch myself to check. I had no idea how long I'd been out, but I was keenly aware that I was lying on a patch of grass. Nearby, I could hear water rushing. It was a river. Black River.

I managed to turn my head to the left slightly and saw my bridge in the distance. I was farther down the riverbank, where the water got really deep and turbulent. White candles had been lit all around me, casting an eerie glow on the overhanging trees above. Just as fear and confusion began to shake me fully alert, Derek kissed my lips and said, "Oh good, you're awake. I was waiting for you, so we could go together."

"Together? Where are we going?" I tried to sit up, but my body wouldn't cooperate, and the pain in my head began throbbing. Suddenly it occurred to me that I hadn't seen Derek drink from the can before he'd handed it to me. Had he drugged it? Drugged me? My body said yes.

He stroked my cheek lovingly. His eyes sparkled in the candlelight. "Nobody knows. But we'll go together. Like Romeo and Juliet. Like we wanted before anybody else got between us."

I looked at him, confused. Why were we at the river? What was going on? "What are you talking about?"

"It'll be easy. Like going to sleep. I'd never let you suffer." Standing, he bent to scoop me into his arms.

"Derek, what are you doing?" My voice sounded small and weak, the way that my body felt.

"I can't lose you. I won't. We're supposed to be together forever." There were tears in his eyes as he looked at me. "And we will now."

"You need help. I want to help you. Where are you taking

me?" He stepped to the edge of the bank, and my heart pounded inside my chest. Drugged, I struggled uselessly. Flashbacks of the night of my attempt filled my mind, and I could see more clearly than ever now that that had been a terrible mistake. I didn't want to die.

Poised there, holding me tight, Derek said, "I love you, Brooke."

I shouted, "Derek, don't! I—"

He stepped forward, and my every nerve jumped in terror. He was going to kill me.

We plunged into the water, and the cold of it shocked my muscles to life. I wrenched as hard as I could to free myself. And when I couldn't, I pulled his hair, clawed his skin, anything I could do to manage to escape. I screamed for help, and Derek's hand closed over my throat, squeezing me into silence. He put his lips to my ear and said, "I know you're scared. It'll all be over soon. And then we'll always be together."

He placed a kiss on my temple and then plunged me into the water. I held my breath until my lungs ached, grabbing at his hands and trying to free myself, but it was useless. I saw bubbles leaving my mouth and nose, climbing to the surface. I felt dizzy, and warmer than I had before he'd plunged me into the water. I was dying. And Derek, the boy who I'd loved, was killing me.

And I wanted to live. I couldn't think of anything that I wanted more than that.

Suddenly I knew what wish I wanted to make. I wished to go on living.

Thinking fast, I let my body go limp and my eyes glaze over. After a moment—one that seemed to stretch on forever—Derek relaxed his grip on me and lifted my head from the water, clutching me to him. He seemed so calm as he bent down and kissed my cold lips. "I love you, Brooke. I'll be with you soon."

Laying me against his chest, facing away from him, he kept his arms around me. I didn't know where he'd gotten the knife, but I watched in silent horror as he plunged the blade into his left wrist. He pulled it toward him, slicing through skin, muscle, and vein. Blood poured out of him. Had it been daylight, I imagined the river would have turned red, if only for a moment. As he began cutting into his right wrist, he stumbled some, woozy from the blood loss.

That's when I made a break for it, slipping his grasp and hurrying to reach the riverbank. As my hand made contact with grass, his wrapped around my ankle. "No, Brooke. Don't leave me!"

The color was leaving his face, and when he blinked

it took effort. He was fading fast. He pulled my leg, but I kicked out with my free leg, hitting him in the jaw with my foot. I crawled up onto the riverbank and got my bearings. I staggered, coughing, and moved as quickly as I could toward home. Behind me, there was silence but for the sound of the river flowing.

I turned back toward the water. The current was taking an unconscious Derek away, and fast. He was going to die if I didn't do something. And though everyone I knew might've said to let him go, that I didn't owe him anything after what he'd done to me, I just couldn't. Derek was a good guy with a troubled life. We all need help sometimes, and right now, Derek needed mine. I dove back into the water, swimming to him as quickly as I could. My arms were sore and still feeling weak, but I pushed on until I reached him. The moment my hand made contact with his body, my mind went back in time to the old man who'd saved me not so long ago. My memory of it was broken into hazy bits and pieces, but I could recall one thing distinctly. He'd said, "It's okay, sweetheart. It's gonna be just fine."

I wanted it to be okay for Derek too. I was living proof that wanting to die, even trying to die, didn't necessarily mean the end of your life.

I pulled his unconscious body up onto the riverbank and checked his pulse. It was weak, but still there. Tearing off fabric from my shirt, I tied makeshift bandages around his wrists. "You'll be okay, Derek. Please, please be okay."

As I ran for help, tears streaked my face. He had to live. He just had to.

CHAPTER TWENTY

It had been a long week of police interviews, emergency therapy sessions with the doc, and pleading with my parents to please, please, please just let it go for one night—forget about what Derek had done and tried to do—and let me hide away in a single moment of a normal life. After a lot of talking, and even more talking with the doc, they'd finally relented. And it was a good thing too. Because the Apothecary looked like his face was melting off.

The play had been going extremely well, with only minor errors, such as Juliet's nurse being late to the stage and Lord Capulet fumbling his lines. Well, that, plus the

Apothecary's inability to stop sweating the makeup off his face. Luckily, Michael had made his way over, patted the Apothecary's face gently with a paper towel to dry it some, and reapplied pancake and setting powder just before he was set to go on. It was a success so far, and the energy between Romeo and Mercutio was incredible—not that I was surprised by that.

Duckie had been perfectly on cue all night, but the moment he'd been nervous about was about to come to fruition. I watched him, holding my breath. Mercutio had just been stabbed. He stumbled, making jokes about being a grave man, and then . . . I could see it in Duckie's demeanor. He wasn't Duckie then. As he fell to the ground, his hand trembling as he reached out to Romeo, who stood stunned, he *was* Mercutio. The audience was completely silent as he cried out, "A plague! On both your houses!"

My heart was in my throat, and I could barely see through the tears welling in my eyes. The audience was stunned. And then they erupted in applause.

Good job, Duckman. Good job.

I watched the rest of the play, but couldn't even look at the stage during the suicide scene. It was too much, too real, too close to home. But when the play was over, the bows taken, the applause given and received, I hunted down Duckie and hugged him tighter than ever. "You were amazing!"

Tucker came up behind Duckie and said, "You really were."

Duckie released me and met Tucker's eyes. "Were?"

Tucker grinned. "Are. Of course."

When they kissed, it seemed so natural, so effortless, so easy. A spot of envy appeared on my heart, but I brushed it away. Duckie and Tucker deserved happiness. So did I, but that didn't have to mean romance. Not now. Not yet. Maybe not for a long time.

"Brooke!" My mom's voice carried all through the backstage. She and Dad hurried over, and she hugged me tight before turning to Duckie and hugging him too. "It was wonderful. Just wonderful."

We both thanked her while Dad held his hand out to Tucker. "So you're the man responsible for the smile on Ronald's face these days. Nice to meet you, son."

Tucker shook his hand, blushing slightly. "Nice to meet you too, sir."

Duckie reached over and took Tucker's hand in his. They chatted with my parents, but I wasn't really listening. Mostly because I was distracted by the sight of Michael holding hands with Claire. They were both smiling. I wasn't sure when or where they'd gotten together, but I was happy for Michael that they had.

Duckie nudged me and said, "So the after party starts in

about a half hour. Are you comin'?"

Before I could answer, my dad slipped twenty bucks into my hand and said, "Home by two."

My mom smiled. "Two-ish."

And even though it was lame, I hugged them both right then and there—without any doubt that we'd make it back to the cabin someday soon.

CHAPTER TWENTY-ONE

It was strange to be back at the inpatient facility. And much better to be a visitor than a patient. But despite the fact that I now understood how important it was that I'd been treated inpatient here, the moment the antiseptic smell filled my nose, I felt a flutter of panic inside my chest.

The fluorescent-yellow visitor badge was stuck to the left side of my jacket. I stared at it, wondering what Derek would say when I saw him. I hadn't seen him in two weeks—the length of his stay here so far. Would he be furious? Sad? Grateful? I had no way of knowing, really. I only knew how I had felt. And if he was anything at all like me, he wouldn't be feeling up for company.

I waited by the desk and did everything I could not to look to my left at the floor where I'd seen Joy and her lifeless eyes. Seeing that floor again would only remind me of her hair spread out on the tiles, her blood pooling underneath her. It was the last thing I needed on a day when I needed to be strong. So I didn't look. Because I was a survivor. And I was determined to keep being one.

The nurse who'd checked me in and given me my badge smiled as she gestured for me to follow. "He hasn't really spoken a word in the two weeks he's been here, so don't expect much. Leave the door open at all times, and if you need anything, you just call. Okay?"

"No problem." I took a deep breath and released it. My lungs felt like they were shaking. Nerves, I guessed.

Through the glass I could see that Derek was sitting on his bed, with his feet on the floor. He wasn't really looking at anything that I could tell, just sitting there with a furious look on his face, fuming.

"Hey, Derek." I moved into the room slowly, not knowing what to expect. I'd only been allowed to visit well before visitors' day due to a recommendation to the inpatient doctors from Dr. Daniels. He thought that Derek might benefit from seeing a friendly face. I wasn't at all certain that Derek considered my face a friendly one.

"They told me that I could come visit today, so I wanted to come check on you, see how you're doing." I stepped closer to him, and he flinched but kept his eyes off me. Taking a chance, I sat on the bed beside him. We stayed there, in tense silence, for several minutes. Derek never moved, never looked at me once. That sick antiseptic smell filled my nose.

I shifted on the bed, the springs squeaking under my weight, until I was facing him. Keeping my voice low, so that it was just between him and me, I said, "It's okay if you don't want to talk. I just wanted to tell you something. Something you might not want to hear."

He was so handsome. Even pale and angry and at the end of his rope, he was lovely. What's more, I knew that the things that he'd done to me had been a desperate attempt on his part to connect with another person and escape his father's abuse. I didn't need the doc to explain that much to me. He'd confirmed it, but I hadn't needed for him to.

I leaned closer, and to my surprise, Derek remained very still as I whispered in his ear.

"I know what it's like." I wet my lips, searching for the right words. Words that I knew I wouldn't have listened to when I'd been inpatient—advice that I never would have taken when I was still in the clutches of my suicidal thoughts. "I know what it's like to be lost in that dark tunnel of depression. It feels hopeless. It feels like nothing will ever be right again. When I was at my lowest, I was absolutely convinced that nobody cared about me and I had no reason to stick around."

His jaw tightened and he balled his hands into fists, but he didn't move or even flinch at my words. "But I was wrong. Life can be really beautiful. Even if happiness is a fragile thing, it's worth fighting for."

In the hall outside the eternally open door, a nurse pushed a medication cart past Derek's room. Memories of my time here echoed in my mind, but from a different perspective now. This was where it had all started—my afterlife, my survival. And this was where Derek's would begin as well.

"I know you never meant to hurt me. And I'm glad you're getting help—even though you may not want it. I'll keep visiting, if you want. Because you need a friend, and I want to be that for you." Ever so gently, I took his left hand in mine and uncurled his fingers. I placed in his palm the best thing that I could ever think to give him—a black origami swan, folded from the note that he'd left on my locker. The one that had simply read "I love you." I stood and placed a soft kiss on his cheek before turning to walk out the door. His cheek, to my surprise, was covered in tears, leaving a salty taste on my lips.

As I walked out of Derek's inpatient room, I knew that this was only the beginning of his journey. I also knew that I was living proof that survival was possible.

Duckie and my parents were waiting outside for me, understanding I might need a little support after seeing Derek. When I approached, Duckie gave me a big hug.

Mom asked, "How is he?"

I looked back at the building—the place I'd considered a prison for six weeks, even though the walls I'd built around myself had been far worse than those of Kingsdale—and said, "He's got a lot of work to do."

Dad nodded and opened the back passenger-side door for me. As I slipped inside the car, he said, "You ready to head to Dr. Daniels's office now?"

Looking up at the third floor, fourth room in, I could see Derek standing there. He was watching us. My heart ached for him in empathy. "Yeah. I have a lot to tell him."

Once we were all buckled in, Dad started the car, and we moved down the road, the inpatient facility shrinking in the side mirror. Smaller and smaller, until it was nothing at all.

ACKNOWLEDGMENTS

To say it's not easy to write a book about depression, suicidal ideation and attempts, self-harm, and a dire need to be loved and understood would be a gross understatement for anyone. But considering that I have experienced all those things personally, I will say that this was the most difficult book that I have ever written. And I absolutely would not have gotten through it without some really amazing people.

My fabulous agent, Michael Bourret, isn't just the best damn literary agent on the planet. He's also an incredible friend. Thank you, MB—for listening, for giving a damn, for sticking with me, for believing in me, for lifting me up. You've given me great advice, listened to me cry over the phone, helped build my outstanding career, and gone out of your way to be there for me. I honestly don't know what I'd do without you.

My incredible editor, Andrew Harwell, deserves a standing ovation every time he walks into a room. Andrew, you've been my friend for a long time, since Vlad was just dipping his toe into high school. I could never trust anyone else to help me dig through my psyche to create a book like this. Thank you for understanding how challenging these subjects are for me and for offering encouragement and kindness. You make me a better writer, which is just about the best gift any editor can give someone. I mean, besides cool mix tapes. ☺

My fantastic team at HarperTeen—you are unmatched in enthusiasm, support, creativity, and awesomeness. Though I can't list everyone here, I want to make an effort to thank at least a few of you. Rosemary, you are such a gem, and I'm so glad that you heard me speak that day at NCTE. Thank you for everything. Olivia Russo, you are the best publicist one could ever hope for. Thank you for taking such good care of me. Epic Reads! You guys are so rad, I just can't even. Thank you for the smiles when I've needed them and for all the fun and support. Oh, and for letting me lick that ARC that one time. Everyone else that I've not named here: I may not remember your names and will likely reintroduce myself a million times whenever I come to the office, but I swear, I adore each and every one of you. Keep being your lovely selves and rockin' the way that you do.

The biggest rebels of all—every damn librarian out there. What can I say to you to express how much you mean to me? It was a librarian who inspired my love of reading. And it was many librarians who first introduced my books to readers everywhere. Thank you! You're always going to hold a very special place in my heart. Please keep doing the magic that you do and spreading that joy of the written word. Readers, even those who don't yet realize that they are readers, are counting on you. So am I.

Many heartfelt thanks to the medical professionals who have and are continuing to help me find a sense of peace while navigating the wild waters of mental illness. It may be my journey, but it's nice to know that there are lighthouses along the way.

The esteemed members of my Minion Horde—my loyal, wacky, beautifully weird, consistently wild, often creepy, forever FANGtastic Minions: I've always told you that I'd be honest with you. This book is further proof of that. Many of you know my story, or at least parts of it. And many more understand what it is to suffer from dark thoughts. Just don't ever forget that when you're way deep inside that pitch-black tunnel of depression . . . I'm right there beside you, holding your hand. All you've gotta do is squeeze. We'll make it to the light at the end every time. And we'll do it together, no matter what. Thank you for listening to me, for sharing your stories with me, and for being a part of something very special. Long live the Minion Horde!

My best friends, A. S. King and Andrew Smith—whenever things get dark, for any of us, it's nice to know that someone is always there to listen . . . or to offer a slice of lemon pie when needed. You two are a rare breed, and I count myself extremely lucky to have you in my life. Mad love to both of you. (Now, get back to work!)

My wonderful son, Jacob—you and I have been through so much together, not all of it good, but we've persevered with strength, stubbornness, and lots of hugs. And while I'll always think of you as that little blond kid, I'm so proud of the man that you've become. I know you have demons of your own, but any time you need me, I'll grab my sword (which will look like Sephiroth's, naturally) and sprint into battle with you. You've always had my back, and I'll always have yours. I love you.

My brilliant daughter, Alexandria—you are consistently the sunshine in my cloudy day. There is a light that follows you everywhere you go, and I know that you will continue to make the world a better place, the way that you've made my life a better life. And when those moments of doubt creep in, you just push them right out again and be Alex out loud.

Never let anyone dull your sparkle. And never forget that we're twins, TWINS, lalalalalala! I love you.

My loving husband, Paul—if anyone in this universe or the next could possibly understand how difficult this book was for me to write, it's you. Because you're the only person who really knows me, who's listened to my secrets and glimpsed the darkness inside. And though I know it must not have been easy, you've stuck by me through it all for over two decades. You're the strongest person I know, my soul mate, my everything. I can never repay you or thank you enough for being a pillar in my life. Never forget how very much I love you—through good times and bad.

I may be a lot of things, but I am not my mental illness. I am, however, loved. But then, as Plato once said, "Love is a serious mental disease."

Thank you for reading. The world is a far better place with you—and me—in it.